About the Author

The lo
reade

argaret Moore actually began her writing career
the age of eight, when she and a friend would
ke up stories together. She also loved to read and
ny years later graduated with a Bachelor of Arts
ree in English Literature. After reading a romance
Kathleen Woodiwiss, Margaret took a course
opular fiction writing and through that, found
ance Writers of America. Three years later, in
, she sold her first historical romance. And the
as they say, is history!

Regency Scandals

Regency Scandal:

Infamous Rogues

MARGARET MOORE

MILLS & BOON

First Published in Great Britain 2020
By Mills & Boon, an imprint of HarperCollins*Publishers*
1 London Bridge Street, London, SE1 9GF

REGENCY SCANDAL: INFAMOUS ROGUES
© 2020 Harlequin Books S.A.

Highland Heiress © 2011 Margaret Wilkins
Highland Rogue, London Miss © 2010 Margaret Wilkins

ISBN 978-0-263-29884-0

MIX
Paper from
responsible sources

FSC
www.fsc.org

FSC™ C007454

This book is produced from independently certified FSC™ paper to ensure responsible forest management.

For more information visit: www.harpercollins.co.uk/green

Printed and bound in Spain
by CPI, Barcelona

HIGHLAND HEIRESS

With many thanks to my parents, my husband and my children for all the support, wisdom and laughs along the way.

Chapter One

Scottish Highlands, 1817

He had been too long in the city, Gordon McHeath thought as he rode along the crest of a hill toward the village of Dunbrachie. He drew in a great, deep breath of the fresh air. After so many years in Edinburgh, he'd forgotten how clean and bracing the air of the Highlands could be. He'd become too used to the smoke and the smells, the noise and the crowds, of a bustling city. Here the silence was broken only by birdsong and the occasional bleating of sheep or lowing of cattle.

The north-facing slope on his left was covered with gorse and bracken, the one on his right with a wood of birch, alders and pine. The needles of the pine were deep green and their scent came to him on the breeze, making him think of Christmas and dark winter nights, although it was only September. The leaves of the other trees were already turning brown and gold, and he guessed the ground beneath would be muddy and damp and thick with mulch. Through the trees he spotted a fast-moving river rushing between rocky banks that probably teemed with salmon in the spring.

Unfortunately, he'd also forgotten how cold a Highland breeze could be, and those heavy, gray clouds in the distance were definitely moving closer. Unless he wanted to be caught in a downpour, he had to get his hired light brown nag moving faster than a walk.

As he went to nudge his horse into a trot, a dog's furious barking broke the country quiet. It wasn't the baying of a hunting hound—more like a watchdog sounding an alarm. A shepherd's dog, perhaps, or a farm dog guarding a crofter's hut.

Gordon rose in his stirrups and looked around. He could see no herd of sheep, no crofter's hut or anything that might require a watchdog.

"Help! Help me!"

The woman's plaintive cry from somewhere in the wood was barely audible over the barking and rushing water, yet there was no mistaking the words, or the desperation.

Punching his heels into the horse's side, Gordon tried to make it leave the road and head toward the sound of the woman and the dog, to no avail, for the beast had the toughest mouth of any horse he'd ever ridden and refused to obey, as if it were more mule than horse.

With a muttered curse, Gordon dismounted, threw the reins over the branch of a nearby bush and began to make his way down the rocky, slippery slope between the trees as quickly as he could.

He tore the sleeve of his three-caped greatcoat on a holly bush. His riding boots were soon covered with mud that dirtied the hem of his coat. His hat got knocked off by a dangling branch he didn't see until it was too late. Reaching down to pick up his hat, he slipped and landed hard and started to slide, until he managed to grab a tree limb.

The dog kept barking, and the woman called out for help again, closer this time, thank God, although he still couldn't see her.

He scrambled to his feet and as he did, he caught sight of the largest, most vicious-looking black dog he'd ever seen at the base of a tall, slender, golden-leafed birch not far from the bank of the river. The dog of no breed Gordon could name was one of the ugliest he'd ever seen, with a huge head and jaw, wide-set eyes and small ears. It stood with legs planted aggressively, growling, a dribble of saliva dripping from its mouth.

Despite that, Gordon was fairly certain it wasn't a mad dog. He'd seen a rabid dog once, frothing and wild-eyed, moving with an uneven sideways gait, and he would never forget it. Nevertheless, he would keep as far from the beast as he could.

"Are you hurt?" The woman's voice came from the same direction as the dog, her accent telling Gordon she was no peasant or shepherdess.

"No," he called back.

Who was she? *Where* was she? He couldn't see

anyone near the dog, or that tree, unless… As he came cautiously closer, he peered up into its branches.

There she was, her arms wrapped around the trunk, standing on a branch that, although she was slender, looked barely able to support her weight.

Despite the circumstance, he couldn't help noticing that she was also exceptionally pretty, with fine features, large, dark eyes and dark curls that peeked out from beneath a daffodil-yellow riding bonnet. Her whole riding habit was that same color of velvet—hardly the outfit of a thief or vagabond.

"I'm all right. Are you injured?" he asked as he considered what to do about the situation, especially that threatening, growling dog.

He had a pistol in his indigo greatcoat, for no man traveled alone and unarmed in this part of the country if he could avoid it, but shooting the animal should be a last resort. It might, after all, only be doing what it was supposed to do, if the young woman had ventured onto private land, for instance.

So instead of taking out his pistol, he bent down and picked up a rock that fit comfortably in the palm of his hand. He'd been a fairly skilled cricket player in his school days, and he prayed his aim hadn't deserted him as he threw the rock at the dog's hindquarters.

It struck the animal hard enough to draw its attention; unfortunately, it didn't run away.

He swiftly searched for another suitable missile that would be heavy enough to make the beast leave, but not to seriously hurt it. A solicitor, he could easily imagine an irate farmer bringing a lawsuit against him for killing his dog that had been dutifully protecting his property.

"This branch is creaking. It's going to break!" the woman cried.

And that would be a long way for her to fall.

He grabbed a rock slightly larger than the last. It was covered with mud and slippery, but he managed to lob it at the dog before it slipped from his gloved hands. It sailed through the air, bits of dirt and debris flying off it before it landed squarely on the dog's back.

Finally the dog fled, loping away through the trees toward the river, where they could hear it splashing.

"Oh, thank you!" the woman cried as Gordon hurried to the foot of the tree. "I was afraid I'd have to stay here all night!"

He could see her better now. She stood balanced on a branch that was only about three inches thick, her arms wrapped around the slim white trunk. In addition to her velvet riding habit, the young woman, who looked to be about twenty, wore tan kid leather gloves and boots. Her skin was fair and smooth, her lips rosy and bow-shaped, and her big coffee-brown eyes regarded him with admiration.

"I'm happy to be of assistance."

"I was lucky you were riding by," she said as she began to climb down with unexpected alacrity, "and equally fortunate I spent so much time climbing in my father's warehouses when I was a girl, or I daresay my fate would be worse."

Warehouses? Of course, her father must be rich. That would explain the velvet. He wondered if she had a mother, brothers, sisters or possibly a fortunate husband.

His curiosity on that point was momentarily suspended when the hem of her dress got caught on a smaller branch, revealing first her booted foot, then her shapely ankle, then her equally shapely, stocking-covered calf....

Good God, what was he doing? Or rather, not doing? "I beg your pardon. Your dress is caught."

"Aye, so it is," the fair unknown replied, tugging it free while a blush added more color to her smooth cheeks. "I had no trouble getting up in the tree when I was afraid that dog would hurt me, but getting down is a different matter."

"Allow me to assist you," he offered when she reached the lowest branch about three feet from the ground.

Although he wasn't quite sure exactly what he was going to do, Gordon stripped off his muddy gloves and shoved them into his pocket before stepping forward.

Not that he should touch her. That wouldn't be proper.

On the other hand, surely these were exceptional circumstances.

She spared him having to come up with a plan by putting her hands on his shoulders. He lifted his arms and grabbed her around the waist. Then she jumped.

Her action was so quick, so confident, he wasn't quite prepared and nearly lost his balance. They both would have fallen to the ground if he hadn't immediately put his arms around her.

He didn't even know her name, yet holding her in his arms felt undeniably...right. No, better than just *right*.

It felt wonderful, as if somehow, this woman was meant to be in his arms.

Which had to be the greatest flight of fancy his logical lawyerly mind had ever taken.

Worse, he was blushing like a schoolboy, although he was nearly twenty-nine. Nor was this the first time he'd ever held a woman in his arms.

"There you are, safe as houses," he said with a smile, trying to sound as if he did this sort of thing every day.

"Thank you for rescuing me. I don't know what I would have done if you hadn't, Mr...?"

"McHeath. Gordon McHeath, of Edinburgh."

"I am in your debt, Mr. Gordon McHeath of Edinburgh."

Never had he been happier to hear the word *debt*.

Then, without a word, without a hint of warning, before he could even realize what she was doing, this woman whose name he didn't even know raised herself on her toes and kissed him.

Her lips were soft, her body lithe and shapely, and her touch sent a rush of fire flashing through his body.

Without thought, acting only on instinct and need, he put his arms around her and pulled her closer. His heartbeat thundered in his ears as he slid his mouth over hers, gliding and grazing, until he coaxed her to let his tongue slip into the moist warmth of her willing mouth. His hands slowly explored the contours of her arching back, caressing her supple spine, her breasts pressed against his rapidly rising and falling chest.

Her hands moved upward, cupping his shoulders from behind, her body relaxing against his.

God help him, he had never been kissed like this. He had never kissed like this. He didn't want to stop kissing like this....

Until he remembered that he was no Lothario, but an Edinburgh solicitor, and she must be from a well-to-do family, perhaps with a father or brothers, or even a husband.

At nearly the same time, she drew back as suddenly as if a wedge had been driven between them. She flushed as red as a soldier's coat and swallowed hard, while he wondered what on earth he should say.

She spoke first. "I'm...I'm sorry, Mr. McHeath," she said, her voice as flustered as her expression. "I don't know what came over me. I'm not usually so... That is, I hope you don't think I often kiss strange men."

He wasn't a strange man, but he knew what she meant. "I don't usually kiss women I haven't been introduced to," he replied.

She moved back even more and ran her gloved hand over her forehead. "It must have been the strain. Or the relief. And gratitude, of course."

Those could be explanations for her actions; what was his excuse for returning her kiss with such fervor?

Loneliness. A heart recently broken, or wounded at least. Her beauty. The feel of a woman's arms around him, although they weren't Catriona McNare's.

Indeed, this bold young woman wasn't at all like the meek and mild Catriona McNare.

"May I ask where you're staying, Mr. McHeath? I'm sure my father will want to meet you, and an invitation to dinner is surely the very least we can do to express our appreciation for your timely assistance."

She spoke of a father, not a husband.

Thank God. "I'm staying at McStuart House."

Her whole manner and attitude altered as if he'd announced he was an inmate of the Edinburgh gaol. Her body stiffened and her luscious lips curled with disdain.

"Are you a friend of Sir Robert McStuart's?" she demanded, her voice as cold as her kiss had been passionate.

"Aye. We went to school together."

Her face reddened not with embarrassment but with obvious rage. What the devil could Robbie have done to make her so angry?

Since it was Robbie, he could think of several things, not the least of which was seduction—and as he knew from legal experience, hell really had no fury like a woman scorned.

"Did he tell you about me?" she demanded, her arms at her sides, her hands curled into fists. "Is that why you thought you could kiss me like that?"

"Sir Robert didn't mention any young women when he invited me here," he answered honestly, trying to remain calm in spite of her verbal attack. "I must also point out that I still don't even know your name, and," he added, "*you* kissed *me*."

Undaunted by his response, she raised her chin and spoke as if she were the queen. "Thank you for your help today, Mr. McHeath, but any friend of Robbie McStuart is no friend of mine!"

"Obviously," he muttered as she turned on her heel and marched away.

The moment Moira MacMurdaugh was out of Gordon McHeath's sight, she gathered up her skirts and ran all the way home.

How could she have been so foolish? And impetuous? And bold? She never should have kissed him. Never should have touched him. She should simply have thanked him and let him go on his way.

When he pulled her closer, she should have broken away at once…even if Gordon McHeath's kiss was like something from a French novel, full of heat and desire and need and yearning.

Worse, she could only imagine what Robbie McStuart would make of this encounter, for surely Gordon McHeath would tell him. Soon more gossip about her would spread through Dunbrachie—and this time, it would be all her fault.

As if that weren't bad enough, it was even more distressing to imagine her father's possible reaction when he found out what she'd done.

He'd kept his pledge to her for nearly six months now—the longest span yet—and it sickened her to think her thoughtless act might cause him to start drinking to excess again.

Perhaps Mr. McHeath wouldn't tell Robbie. After all, he was just as guilty of an improper embrace as she.

"My lady, ye're back! Did ye fall? Are ye hurt?" the gray-haired, stocky head groom cried.

Jem hurried toward her from the entrance to the stables as she entered the yard bordered by a tall stone wall that had once surrounded a castle during the time of Edward Longshanks and William Wallace.

"Yes, I fell, but I'm not hurt. Did Dougal come home?" she asked, speaking of her horse.

"Aye, he's here, the rascal," Jem replied. "We were about to start a search for ye. Your father's going to be that relieved when he sees you."

Cursing herself again for lingering with the handsome Mr. McHeath, even if he was a tall, tawny-haired, strong-jawed, brown-eyed young man who looked like one of those Greek statues she'd seen in London, she hoped she wasn't already too late…until she remembered all the wine and spirits were locked away and she had the only key. It wasn't like Glasgow, where her father had only to go down the street to a tavern.

Nevertheless, she walked quickly through the new part of the manor that had been built by the previous earl, past the kitchen and buttery, the laundry and the servants' dining room.

The delightful, homey smells of fresh bread and roasted beef filled her nostrils, and she felt a pang of nostalgia for the old days, before her father had started to drink heavily and before he'd come into his title and inheritance.

She reached the main floor of the house and the

corridor leading to the library, her father's study and the drawing room. The drawing room was part of the new building; the entrance hall with its dark oak panelling, the study and the library were not. Other rooms had been added in the times between the construction of the castle and the renovation and additions to the manor, so that now the country seat of the Earl of Dunbrachie was an amalgam of every architectural style from the Middle Ages to the Georgian period. She'd spent many hours when they first arrived here exploring all the nooks and crannies, cellars and attics, discovering forgotten pictures and furniture, dust, cobwebs and the occasional dead mouse.

Pausing for a moment to check her reflection in one of the pier glasses that were intended to brighten the otherwise very dark hall, and taking some deep breaths to calm her nerves, Moira removed her bonnet and laid it on the marble-topped side table beneath the mirror, then patted down the smooth crown of her hair.

"Moira!"

She turned to find her father in the door of his study. He was obviously agitated and his dishevelled thick gray hair indicated that he'd run his hands through it repeatedly.

"What happened? Are you hurt?" he asked as she approached. He took hold of her hands as he studied her face and clothes.

She decided the least said about what had happened that day, the better. "I'm quite all right. I took a tumble and Dougal ran off, so I had to walk back."

"I was about to go after you myself."

That explained his riding clothes—which he rarely wore, because he was no horseman, having spent most of his life in offices, mills and warehouses. Thank heavens she'd arrived before he'd gotten on a horse.

"I'm fine, Papa, really," she replied, taking his arm and steering him into his study, which was the one room in the vast hall that seemed most like their old home in Glasgow.

As always, her father's massive mahogany desk was littered with various papers, contracts, ledgers, quills, ink bottles and account books, for although he'd inherited a title and estate, he continued to oversee his business interests back in Glasgow. It looked a mess, but no one was allowed to tidy it, or else, her father claimed, he could never find anything. Older ledgers and account books were on the shelves behind his desk and a threadbare chair stood behind it. She'd been trying to persuade him to recover the chair for years, but he refused that, too, saying it was comfortable just the way it was. The only ornamentation in the room was a bust of Shakespeare sitting on the dark marble mantel that had belonged to one of the other earls.

"I don't think you should be riding alone all over the countryside. What if you'd broken a limb?" her father asked as she sat on the slightly less worn sofa and he leaned back against his desk, wrinkling a paper that was half off the edge.

"I'll be more careful next time. I promise."

"Perhaps you should have a calmer mount—a nice, gentle mare wouldn't be likely to throw you."

Or gallop very fast, either. "Perhaps," she prevaricated, not wanting to upset him more by protesting directly.

"And in future, you must take a groom with you."

Her heart sank as she laced her fingers in her lap. She enjoyed having some time alone, away from the constant presence of all the servants. She supposed wealthy people who'd grown up in such circumstances were used to it; she, as yet, was not.

"You really must start acting more like a lady, Moira."

"I'll try," she said. "There's just so much to remember."

And so many restrictions.

"With rank comes both privileges and duty," her father reminded her.

Moira was well aware of that. Fortunately, not everything some would consider a duty was onerous to her.

"The school building is coming along nicely, Papa. You should come and see. And I've sent out the advertisement for a teacher," she said, turning the subject away from her fall and its aftermath, and especially Gordon McHeath, silently vowing to stay far away from handsome strangers even if they looked like a maiden's dream, kissed like Casanova and came charging to the rescue like William Wallace attacking the English.

His expression pensive, her father walked round his desk and shuffled some papers before he spoke again. "You do realize, Moira," he began without looking at her, "that not everyone in Dunbrachie is in favor of your charitable endeavor? Even parents whose children will benefit are afraid you'll be filling their heads with visions of futures that can't possibly come to pass."

"That's because they don't yet appreciate the value of an education," she staunchly replied. "I expected some opposition. There always is when something is new and different. But once they see the value of being able to read and write and the opportunities it will afford their children, surely their opposition will melt away."

"I hope so," her father replied, glancing up at her. "I truly hope so. I would never forgive myself if something happened to you."

She knew how much her father loved her and wanted her to be safe and happy. A more selfish, ambitious man would never worry about her as he did, or try to keep his promise not to overimbibe, or come to her with such a stricken, sorrowful expression when he discovered the truth about the man she had agreed to marry, and the things he'd done. She didn't doubt that it had been almost as upsetting for her father to learn the true nature of her fiancé and have to tell her about it as it had been for her to hear it.

She hurried to embrace him. "We'll look after each other, Papa," she said with fervent determination, "as we've always done, in good times and bad."

So she said, although she just as fervently hoped the bad times were at an end.

Chapter Two

Built in the Palladian style of granite and with a slate roof, McStuart House nestled on the side of the hill overlooking the village of Dunbrachie. The first time Gordon had been there as a lad of twelve he'd been awed into silence by the magnificent and spacious house and its army of servants. The last time he'd visited here, about five years ago, he'd counted the windows and discovered there were thirty-eight, front and back, and not including the French doors that led to the terrace from the drawing room and library.

But the architectural details of Robbie's home, which he'd inherited on the death of his father three years ago, were not uppermost in Gordon's mind as he approached this day. Nor were the thickening rain clouds.

He was thinking about that young woman, and Robbie—not that he wanted to think of them together, in any way.

He didn't want to believe that his first assumption about the cause of her rage—a love affair gone wrong—was the correct one, so he tried to come up with other explanations for her anger.

Maybe there had been a family business venture involving Robbie that went awry. Robbie was not the most responsible of men, and he had no head for figures—except those of women—so it could well be that some sort of transaction or bargain had turned out badly.

Perhaps there was a sister or a cousin or a friend Robbie had flirted with and she was angry because she was jealous.

Whatever the explanation, as he neared the large portico at the front of McStuart House and the first drops of rain began to fall, he decided not to mention the encounter to Robbie. He didn't want to hear Robbie's account or explanations, especially if he and that bold, beautiful young woman had been lovers. He wanted to rest, and to try to forget Catriona.

He tied the horse to the ring on one of the columns and hurried up the three wide steps to the equally wide front door with a stained glass fanlight above. The door swung open to reveal a tall, austere butler Gordon didn't recognize.

"Mr. McHeath, I presume?" the older man said in a refined English accent.

"Aye," Gordon answered, giving his coat and hat to the liveried footman who appeared beside the butler.

"Sir Robert is expecting you in the drawing room."

Gordon nodded and hurried inside, making his way to

the drawing room through the imposing foyer with walls covered with the horns of stags and rams, spears, pikes, swords and armor. Beyond the drawing room and wide double staircase were several other rooms, such as the library where he and Robbie had played at soldiers when they were younger, and a billiard room they'd used when they were older. There were at least three bedrooms on the main level and twelve above, and servants' quarters above that, on the uppermost level. He still had no idea how many smaller rooms existed below stairs, where the kitchen, laundry, pantry, buttery, wine cellar, servants' parlor, servants' dining room and various other rooms necessary for the running of the house were located.

When he entered the drawing room, he immediately spotted Robbie standing by the French doors leading to the flagstone terrace where the rain was now falling in earnest. Looking out over the garden that had been designed by Inigo Jones, his friend stood with his head lowered, one hand braced against the door frame, the other loosely holding an empty wineglass.

That was such an unusual pose for Robbie, Gordon wasn't sure if he should disturb him or not, so he took a moment to survey the room. Nothing seemed to have changed since the last time he was here. The walls were still papered in that unusual shade of ochre, the gilded furniture was still covered with the same dark green velvet. The same portraits of long-dead ancestors hung in the same places, the same landscapes in theirs. Even the books on the side tables looked as if they were the ones that had been there five years ago. Everything was clean, with not a speck of dust to be seen, but otherwise, it was as if time had stood still.

Until Robbie turned around.

What the devil had happened to him? He looked as if he'd aged a decade, and a hard-lived decade at that. His face was pale and gaunt and there were dark semicircles beneath his bloodshot blue eyes. While his body had always been slim, now it looked almost skeletal. Only his thick, waving fair hair appeared unchanged.

As Gordon tried not to stare, Robbie set his wineglass on the nearest table and walked toward him smiling.

At least his smile was the same, merry and charming, and a spark of vitality was in his voice as he cried, "Gordo, you old bookworm! I thought you'd never get here! But I never should have doubted you'd arrive after sending me word you'd come, should I? Always dependable, that's Gordo!"

Gordon had always detested that particular version of his name, yet he was far too concerned about his friend's state of health to be annoyed. "I ran into a bit of trouble on the far side of the village," he said dismissively before asking with more concern, "How are you, Robbie?"

"I've been a little under the weather," his friend admitted as he reached out to shake Gordon's hand.

"Nothing serious, so stop staring at me like an undertaker taking mental measurements," he finished with a laugh, his grip strong and firm. "Just a little too much of the juice of the grape last night."

That would certainly explain his appearance. And Robbie had never been much of an eater. But it was his hearty handshake that convinced Gordon there was nothing seriously amiss with his health.

"Let's have a drink. I'm sure you need one," his friend continued as he went to a cabinet and poured some amber-colored liquid into two glasses. "The roads around here can make for a damned uncomfortable ride."

Although Gordon suspected Robbie had already been drinking more than was good for him, he was tired and thirsty and accepted the whiskey. "Thank you."

Robbie downed his neat. Still holding the glass, he ambled toward the ornately carved hearth. "I suppose you were surprised to get my invitation."

"I was delighted," Gordon truthfully replied. And very happy to have a good reason to be away from Edinburgh for a while.

Robbie fingered his glass and looked down at the empty interior. "Yes, well, I confess my motives weren't completely selfless. I've had a bit of trouble, Gordo."

Involving a beautiful young woman whose passion could send a man reeling? God, he hoped not!

Nevertheless, he managed to calmly reply. "I see. What sort of trouble?"

Robbie gestured toward the sofa closest to him. "Sit down and I'll tell you all about it—or do you want a bite to eat first? I've got a new cook, a Frenchman. Can't understand half of what he says, but the food's wonderful."

No doubt costly, too, but the McStuarts had been rich since the Jacobite Rebellion, when they'd switched churches and allegiances to their advantage as easily as most men changed trousers. Not the most honorable of heritages, Robbie used to say, but it had kept the family solvent ever since.

"No, thank you. I'd rather hear about you," Gordon replied as he sat down.

Robbie poured himself another whiskey, while Gordon twisted his half-full glass in his hand and waited.

"Well, Gordo, I suppose it had to happen eventually," Robbie began, sighing as he leaned against the cabinet, holding his glass loose in his fingers with the same casual ease he always displayed, even when called before the tyrannical headmaster at the school where they'd met when they were ten years old. "I've had my heart broken at last, old chum. Smashed. Shattered. Wrecked and ruined by a cold and stubborn woman."

A romantic affair gone wrong then.

Even though there was still the chance that Robbie's heart had been broken by a woman who didn't wear a yellow velvet riding habit, Gordon wished he'd taken another route, so he'd never have had that passionate, disastrous encounter.

"Yes, Gordo, it's true. I fell in love—deeply, completely in love. And I thought she loved me, too, so I asked her to marry me."

That was even more shocking. Robbie had certainly professed to being in love before—many times, in fact—but as far as Gordon knew, he'd never gone so far as to propose.

What, then, had gone wrong?

"Yes, I was actually ready to put my neck into the

matrimonial noose—and she accepted. Seemed only too happy, in fact. We announced it at a ball at her father's house."

"Her father being…?"

"The Earl of Dunbrachie."

Gordon tried to keep his expression suitably sober, although his heart fairly leaped with relief. *Her* father was a merchant or manufacturer who owned warehouses, not a titled nobleman.

"A fine match for us both, and then barely a fortnight later, she tells me she won't marry me after all."

No wonder Robbie looked exhausted. He, too, had spent many a night these past few months tossing and turning, thinking about his feelings for Catriona McNare. What he'd done and not done, said or should have said. Although he would never have sought solace in a bottle as he feared Robbie had been doing, he could certainly appreciate the inclination to want to drown his sorrows and seek the comforting company of an old friend. "I'm very sorry, Robbie."

"I knew I could count on you to be sympathetic," Robbie said with a grin. "And in one way, I suppose I should count myself lucky. Do you know what her father was before he inherited the title? A wool merchant. A very rich wool merchant, but a wool merchant nonetheless."

The ceiling collapsing on Gordon's head couldn't have shocked him more. A rich wool merchant would have warehouses, or access to them.

"He was so distantly related to the late earl," Robbie continued without looking at his silent friend, "it came as a shock to everybody—including him, I gather. And Moira herself can be eccentric. She has a positive mania about educating the poor. Wants to build a school for the children of Dunbrachie, although what they'd do with an education I have no idea. It's not like most of the men in Dunbrachie want a school, either."

If it was the same woman—and Gordon clung to the fast-diminishing hope that he was still jumping to the wrong conclusion—why had she broken the engagement? To be sure, Robbie could be impulsive and wasn't prone to planning, but he was handsome, rich and titled, loyal and good-natured. Many a nobleman's daughter could, and did, do worse.

"It would have been upsetting if she'd refused when I'd asked her, but I daresay I would have gotten over it soon enough. After all, there are plenty of other attractive, rich and nobly born women who would welcome my attention."

Whoever the woman was, Gordon could certainly understand Robbie's bitterness. Still, there was an arrogance in his tone that made it more difficult to sympathize with his friend. On the other hand, would he not have sounded so bitter and defensive if someone had asked him what was troubling him lately, too?

Robbie walked to the French doors, turned on his heel and made a sweeping gesture with the hand holding his empty glass. "Who does Moira MacMurdaugh think she is, that she can make a fool out of Sir Robert McStuart? She's the fool if she thinks I'm simply going to let her humiliate me. That's why I need your help, Gordo." He straightened his shoulders and a triumphant gleam came to his bloodshot eyes. "I want to sue Lady Moira MacMurdaugh for breach of promise."

Now it was as if the floor had given way, too. "You want to sue this woman for breach of promise?" Gordon repeated.

"Exactly."

Gordon forced himself to try to forget about the woman who might or might not be the one he'd kissed, and think like the solicitor he was. Robbie clearly hadn't considered all the ramifications of starting a legal action that was generally the province of women. "I can appreciate that you're upset—"

"Upset? I'm not upset," Robbie snapped, setting his glass down on an ebony-inlaid side table so hard, Gordon expected it to break. "I simply want her to understand that she can't go around accepting proposals and rejecting them out of hand. Or don't you think I have a case?"

Now things were getting even more difficult. Robbie might have a case, but there were other considerations he should take into account, as Gordon proceeded to explain. "If the engagement was public knowledge, you do have some cause of action. However, there's something else you might want to think about first, Robbie. Dunbrachie is a small village, but this sort of legal activity will likely come to the attention of a wider circle, and probably the press, at least in Scotland. Your—" he hesitated, and chose a word other than *humiliation* "personal concerns may well become gossip fodder, splashed about the papers and discussed by complete strangers.

"Would it not be better to simply forget what happened? After all, as you yourself said, there have always been women eager for your attention.

"I'm sure you'll find love again," he finished, voicing a wish he harbored for himself, a wish that had suddenly seemed far more possible when he'd looked up and seen a beautiful woman trapped in a tree.

"You're rather missing the point, Gordo," Robbie said as he threw himself onto the sofa. "I'm not just doing this for myself. I'm doing it for all the other poor sods whose hearts she might break."

He turned his head and regarded Gordon with a measuring, sidelong look. "If I were a woman in such circumstances, you'd take the case, wouldn't you?"

"Perhaps," Gordon replied. He wasn't really sure what he'd do. However, he truly believed it would do Robbie more harm than good to sue. "What reason did she give for breaking the engagement? She did have a reason, I assume."

Scowling, Robbie sat up. "She said she didn't love me," he replied with more than a hint of defiance, as if such a thing were too ludicrous to be credible.

Given Robbie's experience with the fairer sex, he might be excused for thinking so. Nevertheless... "Perhaps it's for the best then," Gordon replied, repeating the same thing he'd been telling himself ever since he'd met Catriona McNare's fiancé.

Robbie's brows lowered and his mouth got that stubborn set Gordon well remembered. "She said she could *never* love a man like me."

A man like Robbie, who was handsome and charming

and a good friend? "What on earth did she mean by that?"

Robbie jumped to his feet and strode to the window. "It means she doesn't understand how the upper class lives. I haven't committed any crime. I haven't done anything every nobleman in Scotland or England and certainly France hasn't done before me. She claims to be a lady, yet she broke the engagement over a trifle."

If he had done something to cause her to change her mind, that made a difference. "I think you'd better tell me what exactly this 'trifle' was."

Robbie didn't answer right away. First he marched to the cabinet and poured himself another drink, making Gordon wonder if too much drink was the trifle, and if so, it was indeed no trifle. No woman of sense wanted to marry a drunkard.

"If I'm to act as your solicitor in this matter, Robbie, I have to know all the details," Gordon said quietly, beginning to feel a bit sorry that he'd accepted Robbie's invitation.

He thought his friend had asked him there because they were friends and it had been a long time since they'd seen each other, not because he needed legal advice, yet now there was a possibility he was going to get embroiled in a case he'd prefer to avoid.

Robbie gulped down his whiskey and when he looked at Gordon again, he appeared even more haggard, as if telling the truth was physically painful. Nevertheless, he smiled his merry, charming smile—only this time, it seemed more like a death's-head grin to Gordon.

"No need to look so stern, Gordo. It was only a

dalliance with one of the maids, the sort of thing that goes on all the time."

He should have guessed it would be something like this. Robbie had always had "high spirits," as their headmaster had called it when Robbie had been discovered with one of the maids at school. Indeed, he'd been famous for his liaisons and the envy of every boy in school.

But that was in the world of males. He could easily imagine—and sympathize with—a potential bride's dismay at learning of her future husband's lustful activities with a servant. "Did you assure her you'd be faithful once you were married?"

Robbie looked at Gordon as if he'd suggested giving up food and drink. "No. Why would I? Why should I?"

Gordon's heart sank. "Because you were going to make such a promise when you said your marriage vows."

"Gad, Gordo, don't tell me you, with your profession, are naive enough to think any man's really going to be faithful to his wife?"

"I've met several who are," Gordon replied, recalling some of the happily married clients who'd passed through his offices.

Robbie slouched onto an armchair near the sofa and frowned like a petulant child. "Sometimes I forget you're…" He fell silent and picked at a bit of lint on his lapel with his slender fingers that had never done a day's work.

"Not of your class?" Gordon finished for him.

His friend blushed, the fire of his anger apparently quenched as he regarded Gordon with dismay, and the first sign of genuine remorse. "I'm sorry, Gordon." He spread his hands in a gesture of surrender. "I'll be perfectly honest with you. Yes, I dallied with one of the maids, but I never thought a fiancée or even a wife would really mind. I mean, you were at school. You heard the other boys talking about their fathers' and brothers' mistresses and lovers. It's accepted in our world, or at least condoned. It was just a maid, after all. It's not like I was keeping a mistress in the house. And I turned her out as soon as Moira learned about her."

While Gordon was certainly well aware that many rich and titled men treated women like their personal toys to be used or discarded at will, he didn't approve of that selfish behavior. And if Robbie thought hearing that the maid had lost her place because of their liaison was going to increase Gordon's sympathy for his cause, he was even more mistaken. Gordon had helped too many servants who'd been seduced and cast out by their employers, suing for back wages at the very least, to have any sympathy for a master who took advantage of one.

In spite of his efforts to keep a blank countenance, his face must have betrayed something of his feelings, for Robbie's next words had more than a tinge of self-defence. "It's not as if the maid wasn't willing. She was, I assure you. *Very* willing. Indeed, I think *she* seduced *me*."

Gordon had heard this sort of excuse many times,

too. "You were her master, Robbie. She might have felt she couldn't refuse."

"Of course she could!" Robbie retorted, hoisting himself to his feet. "I'm hardly some kind of brutal ogre."

No, he wasn't. Nevertheless...

"And I was honest enough not to make a promise to Moira that I wasn't going to keep. But did she appreciate that? No, she looked at me as if I'd committed murder."

Robbie ran his hand through his hair before starting for the cabinet again. "Maybe if she hadn't been so angry..." Wrapping his hand around the decanter, he shook his head. "Oh, I don't know what I would have done if she'd been calmer." He walked away without pouring another drink and went to the fireplace. He picked up the poker and vigorously stirred the coals, sending ash swirling upward.

"Maybe instead of suing her, you should be grateful," Gordon said quietly. "If you'd married her and strayed, and then she found out—"

"We would have been married and there would have been nothing she could do about it. She would have learned to accept that it's a nobleman's privilege, as my mother did and her mother before her."

Gordon didn't like what he was hearing. It smacked of brutal arrogance, of utter selfishness and a complete disregard for the feelings of another human being, the sort of attitude that spurred him to find justice for the weak and abused and cheated, and especially for women, who had so few rights under the law.

Rising, he went to face his friend, the better to see

his face and read his expression, for eyes often said what words did not.

As a certain young lady's eyes had spoken of desire before they'd kissed.

"What if your wife took a lover? Would you say then it was simply what people of your class do?"

Robbie clenched his jaw for the briefest of moments before he answered. "Of course. As long as I had an heir and a spare, my wife could take as many lovers as she liked."

Robbie marched across the room to the cabinet, then turned to face his friend. "Obviously, I should have lied to you, and her. I should have said that of course I would be faithful. That I'd never even look at another woman.

"But I didn't. So if you'd rather not represent me in this, I'll find another solicitor who will. With you or without you, Gordo, I'm suing Moira McMurdaugh for breaking our engagement."

Gordon regarded Robbie steadily. While Robbie never made any reference to what had happened at school, Gordon could never forget what he owed Robbie McStuart.

And if it was the same woman he'd rescued from the tree and kissed?

He still owed Robbie his career. "Of course I'll represent you, Robbie."

Chapter Three

Three days later, Moira leaned over the pedestal table in the book-lined library, studying the builder's drawings of the future school, as well as his notations. She wanted to be sure that she was right before she addressed the prosperous middle-aged man standing before her with his thumbs in his vest pockets, rocking back and forth on his heels.

She was, but having dealt with tradesmen for many years, she didn't begin with a direct accusation. That would only lead to confrontation, arguments, denials and, eventually, the pronouncement that women couldn't be expected to understand business or the arithmetic that went with it.

"Mr. Stamford," she began, "I must confess that I find your estimates rather…excessive."

The plump man merely smiled with frustrating con-descension. "Perhaps, my lady, we should wait for your father's return from Glasgow. He'd due back today, is he not?"

"Yes, he is," she replied, hoping with all her heart he would return as promised and hadn't met any of his friends who had, in the past, led him astray. "However, the school is my responsibility, not his."

Her statement didn't appear to make any difference to the builder, for the man continued to regard her as if she were merely an overgrown child, and one incapable of understanding simple addition and multiplication, too. "I'm sure, as a former man of business, your father will be able to comprehend the figures better than a young lady. You mustn't trouble your pretty head with such things as measurements and structure, square feet and raw materials," Mr. Stamford continued with that same insufferable patronage.

"Perhaps *you* don't understand, Mr. Stamford, that as the daughter of a man of business who's been keeping household accounts for ten years, ever since my mother died, I'm not incapable of calculating totals and expenditures," she said, determined not to let this man think he could flatter her into believing that his estimates of the costs of materials were reasonable when they were so obviously not. "Nor, having had considerable work done on this house, am I ignorant of the costs involved when refurbishing a building. I find your estimate of the price for the necessary materials for the school and labor excessive. You're building a school, after all, not a manor house."

The man's cheeks puffed out with an annoyed huff. "Far be it from me to contradict a lady. However, if one wishes to use the best materials—and I was under the impression you did—then one has to pay accordingly."

"I want the best for the purpose," she clarified. "The prices you're quoting would seem to indicate you're using wood and stone more suitable for a cathedral than a village school. We recently had the dining room of this house panelled in mahogany brought especially from Jamaica, Mr. Stamford, and the price of that mahogany was less than this quotation for the oak ceiling beams of the main schoolroom. I fail to see how that is possible, unless the oak is gilded."

The builder's face turned as red as lip rouge. He reached for the plans spread on the table and began to roll them up, the pages crackling and crinkling with his swift action. "If you don't like the plans or the cost, my lady, you can always hire another man!"

"Unless you can provide me with a more reasonable quote, I may have to," Moira replied, not a whit disturbed or intimidated by his bluster, "although I'd hate to think you've done so much work for nothing."

"Nothing?" the man almost shrieked. "I expect to be paid for the time and effort I've already—!"

"Of course," she smoothly interrupted, "it would be a pity to have this assignment come to a premature end."

"Like some women's engagements?" he retorted.

Moira managed to control the rage that spiralled through her. She wanted to dismiss him on the spot, but that would lead to a delay, which would surely upset her father. That was always something to be avoided, lest he be tempted to break his vow.

"It would also be unfortunate that you wouldn't be able to brag about working for the Earl of Dunbrachie's daughter anymore, as I believe you already have."

Or so the butler had informed her, having had it from the footman, who'd been in the village tavern the night before last.

The man's gaze finally faltered and he put the plans back on the table. "Aye, yes, well, perhaps I was a tad hasty, my lady," he said in a conciliatory tone, "and I'm a hot-tempered fellow. I suppose we could use less oak and more pine, and maybe I don't have to buy so much slate for the roof."

Despite his change of manner and her relief that things could proceed as planned, there was something else she considered important to make clear. "I don't want any corners cut. The building must be safe and sound."

"That school will be so well built, it'll still be standing a hundred years from now," he assured her.

"Excellent, Mr. Stamford," she conceded, "and if I see more realistic figures, I see no need to tell my father about our difference of opinion. Now I give you good day, sir. I'll be by to check the progress of the school later in the week."

"Yes, my lady. Goodbye, my lady, and I'm sure I'll be able to find ways to economize, my lady."

With that, he bustled out of the library as if he couldn't get away fast enough, which was probably the case. She was just as relieved to see him go. She was well aware that her broken engagement to Sir Robert McStuart was no secret, but it was nevertheless galling to have it flung into her face.

It was even more galling to realize that Gordon McHeath had surely heard about her broken engagement by now, and from Robbie McStuart, too, she thought as she walked around the room, brushing her fingertips over the leather spines of the books that had so delighted her when they'd first arrived. Her former fiancé would undoubtedly paint what had happened between them in the worst possible way, making light of his own transgressions and describing her as some sort of narrow-minded, unsophisticated bumpkin.

If only she could stay as angry and indignant as she'd been when she found out the man who had come to her rescue was Robbie McStuart's friend. Unfortunately, as time had passed, she found herself thinking less of his friendship with Robbie and more of the passion she'd felt in his arms. The excitement. The wish that his embrace would never end. She remembered Gordon McHeath's smile, his gentlemanly demeanor and the sight of him charging down the hill like a knight errant. Even more vividly, she recalled the urge to kiss him that she hadn't been able to fight, his passionate response, the sensation of his arms around her and his lips covering hers, seeking, demanding, wanting….

"I beg your pardon, my lady," the butler intoned from the door. "A gentleman wishes to see you." He held out a silver salver with a card upon it. "He says it's a legal matter, my lady."

Legal matter? "Did you tell him the earl isn't at home?"

"I did, and he said it doesn't involve the earl, my lady. His business is with you."

Perhaps it had something to do with the school, although she couldn't imagine what. She went to the door and took the card. She glanced at it, then stared.

Gordon McHeath, Solicitor, Edinburgh.

Robbie McStuart's friend was a solicitor? Even so, what could he possibly want with her? It couldn't be because of that kiss…could it? That hadn't violated any law that she was aware of.

Perhaps it had something to do with the dog that had chased her. "Show him in, please."

Smoothing down her skirt and tucking a stray lock of hair behind her ear, determined to keep the conversation coolly business-like, she perched primly on an armchair covered in emerald-green damask near the hearth.

Mr. McHeath appeared on the threshold. He wasn't dressed in his caped greatcoat and hat; otherwise, his clothing was similar, down to his riding boots. Without his hat, his tawny hair waved like ripples on a lake, and he was definitely as handsome and well built as she remembered.

He hesitated, and a look passed over his face that made her think he was about to leave just as abruptly.

He didn't. His visage slightly flushed, as she suspected hers must be, he came farther into the room, his expression solemn to the point of grimness.

Commanding herself to be calm and detached, and above all to forget she had ever kissed him, she said,

"So, Mr. McHeath, what is this legal matter that has brought you here today?"

His gaze swept over the room and furnishings, lingering for a moment at the pedestal table with the drawings still on top before he came to a halt and pulled a folded document from the pocket of his navy blue jacket.

"I've come on behalf of Sir Robert McStuart regarding the matter of your broken engagement," he said, his voice just as coldly formal as hers had been. "He's bringing an action against you for breach of promise."

Moira stared at him in stunned disbelief. "Breach of…? He's *suing* me?"

"Yes." McHeath took a deep breath, like a man about to dive into frigid water. "He's seeking damages in the amount of five thousand pounds."

With a gasp as if she'd landed in that frigid water, Moira jumped to her feet. "I don't believe it! Five thousand pounds? Five *thousand* pounds?"

"I agree it's a considerable sum, but you must be aware of the damage your change of mind has done to his reputation. He feels he should be duly compensated."

"*His* reputation?" she repeated, her hands balling into fists, her whole body shaking with righteous indignation. "What *was* his reputation, that he should set such store on it? And what about mine? Don't you think mine has suffered just as much, if not more?"

The solicitor didn't seem the least nonplussed. "Then perhaps, my lady, you should offer a sum to settle before the matter goes before a judge."

"You want me to pay him off? Are you mad?" she demanded, appalled as well as angry. "I'm not going to give that libertine a ha'penny. If there's anyone at fault for what happened, it's him. Didn't he tell you why I broke the engagement?"

"He told me that you informed him that you no longer loved him," the solicitor replied, still standing as stiff and straight as a soldier on a parade square. "He said that you were angry about his dalliance with a maid, and because he refused to assure you he would be faithful in the future."

All that was true and yet..." *A* dalliance? Only one?"

Finally, something seemed to bring a spark of passionate life back to Gordon McHeath's eyes. Unfortunately, the change lasted only an instant before he resumed that statuelike demeanor. "Yes, only one."

"In addition to the chambermaid at McStuart House, there were three girls at his family's weaving mill and the scullery maid in his town house in Edinburgh that I know about," she informed him. "There may very well be more. He also drinks, Mr. McHeath, far too much. He managed to keep that hidden from me for quite some time, but fortunately not long enough for me to go through with the marriage. I have long vowed that I would never marry a sot."

McHeath glanced down at the toes of his boots, so she couldn't see his face. When he raised his eyes to her, his expression was again that blank mask, as if they'd never even met, let alone kissed. Indeed, she could hardly believe this was the same man who'd come rushing so gallantly to her rescue and who'd kissed her with such fervent passion.

"It was your duty to find out about the man proposing marriage before you accepted him, my lady," he said. "Apparently you did not. You could have asked for more time to consider. You did not. You also said that you no longer loved him. This suggests you not only felt a moral indignation when you learned of his liaisons, you experienced an inner revelation concerning the depth of your own feelings. That is something over which my friend had absolutely no control. You alone are responsible for that and as such, Sir Robert has some justification for his claim.

"More importantly from a legal point of view, you entered into a verbal contract that was publicly announced, and you broke that contract."

"Good God," she gasped, aghast at his cool and condemning response and backing away from him as if he held a loaded pistol. "You're absolutely serious about this!"

"I assure you, my lady, I would never jest about a lawsuit."

That she could well believe. Indeed, at this moment, she could well believe he never made a jest or joke about anything.

But he *was* the man who had saved her from that dog, so surely he could have some sympathy for her feelings, and her decision. "Whatever I *thought* I felt, I realized I was wrong and acted accordingly. Would you really have me marry a man I no longer cared for and could no longer even respect? Would you really want me—or any woman—to tie herself to such a man under those conditions?"

The attorney had the grace to blush as he steadily met her gaze. "No, I wouldn't, but again I remind you, my lady, that whatever Sir Robert's faults, it was your responsibility to discover them before you accepted his proposal."

Was the man made of marble? Had he no heart? "Surely a judge will side with me and agree that I was right to end the engagement."

"Judges are men, my lady. He may well agree that Sir Robert deserves to be compensated."

Unfortunately, he had a point. Men made the laws, and men upheld them.

And what about Gordon McHeath, who had seemed so kind and chivalrous? "Do *you* condone his behavior, Mr. McHeath?"

He didn't look away. "Condone? No, I do not. But I was not raised as he was, by parents who believed their birth and station meant certain social mores didn't apply to them."

"So even if you don't agree with what he's doing, you would defend him?"

"I represent him."

With a horrible sick feeling in the pit of her stomach, she thought of another reason he might believe a judge would side with Robbie. "Did you tell him that we kissed?"

Although Mr. McHeath continued to regard her dispassionately, his cheeks reddened a little more. "I saw no need to mention that particular act to Sir Robert, or anyone else. I hope you have been similarly reticent. It does neither of us credit."

Her heart began to beat again, albeit erratically, for despite his explanation for his reticence, she sensed he wasn't as sorry or ashamed as he claimed to be.

Neither, she realized, was she—even now. Wanting to see if she was right, she pressed him for more of an explanation. "It would help your case, would it not?"

"I saw no need to provide more evidence when I had hoped you would be reasonable and offer a sum in settlement so that the case need not proceed."

In spite of his evenly spoken reply, she sidled a little closer, so that she could see into his eyes, the better to gauge his true response. "Given that Sir Robert seems to be selective with the facts, are you aware that five thousand pounds was to be the amount of my dowry?"

No, he hadn't known that. She could see the surprise he tried to hide. "Obviously he wants the dowry he didn't get," she observed.

Mr. McHeath swiftly recovered from his surprise. "Whatever his reasons, that is the sum he feels is appropriate compensation."

"*I* feel he's not entitled to anything, and nothing you say will ever make me change my mind."

Mr. McHeath inclined his head. "Very well, my lady, and since we seem to be unable to come to any agreement, I shall bid you good day."

She shouldn't feel any regret when he said those words. She shouldn't be sorry he was leaving. After all, she barely knew him, and he was working for Robbie.

"You may also tell Sir Robert that I do not and never will regret breaking our engagement. If anything, his petty, vindictive action further convinces me that I was right to do so," she said as she went to the hearth and tugged the bellpull beside it. "Good day, Mr. McHeath. Walters will show you out."

When Gordon returned to McStuart House, he immediately went in search of his host, although every step seemed an effort. He wasn't looking forward to having to relay Lady Moira's response any more than he'd been to confront her. Indeed, he'd been seriously tempted to leave without revealing the purpose of his visit when he saw that Lady Moira was the woman he'd helped and kissed, but gratitude and duty demanded that he do what he'd been asked to do. Now Robbie would want to know what had happened.

It would be far better for all concerned if they each simply went their own way, and let the past stay in the past. Unfortunately, despite his best efforts, Robbie was determined to have his day in court, and be compensated for the blow to his pride.

Even more unfortunately, Lady Moira wasn't the only person in Dunbrachie who could be faulted for not knowing more about a man before entering into an agreement with him. He should have been much more wary of agreeing to represent Robbie in a legal matter, especially after he'd noticed how much Robbie drank that first afternoon.

He finally found Robbie in the last room he thought to look—the library. Unlike the earl's library, this one had an air of musty neglect, and many of the volumes weren't even real books. In fact, Gordon was rather sure neither Robbie nor his father had read a book in its entirety after they left school.

The dark draperies added to a sense of genteel decay, and the portraits in this room all seemed to be of people in a state of chronic indigestion.

Its only saving grace—and perhaps its appeal for Robbie—was the large windows opening to the terrace. Or maybe its isolation from the other rooms, and thus its silence, explained why he had gone there.

Naturally Robbie wasn't reading a book. He wasn't even awake. He lay sprawled on his back on one of the worn, silk-covered sofas, his right arm thrown over his face, his left crossed over his chest and an empty bottle of port on the floor beside him.

Chapter Four

Gordon sighed heavily and leaned back against one of the shelves. Whatever Robbie thought, Lady Moira was right to be wary of marrying a man who drank so much. In his practice he'd seen too many marriages fall into bitter ruin and too many families destroyed because of drink.

Robbie's blue eyes flickered open. "Gordo! You're back!" he muttered as he lurched to a sitting position. "Why didn't you wake me?"

"I'm only just returned," he replied. He came farther into the room and sat in a wing chair opposite Robbie. He nodded at the bottle on the floor. "Isn't it a little early for that?"

Robbie sighed and rubbed his temples as he hunched over. "My head ached, so I had a little drink for medicinal purposes."

"A *little* drink?"

"Aye, just enough to put me to sleep."

"Perhaps your head ached from imbibing too much last night," Gordon suggested, trying to keep his tone nonjudgmental.

Robbie frowned. "You're not my nursemaid."

"No, I'm not. I'm your friend, and I'm worried about you."

Robbie slid down until he was lying on his back, his head resting on the arm of the sofa. "If I'm drinking a little more than usual, it's because that's the only way I can sleep most nights."

Gordon wondered what his "usual" amount of drinks per day would be, then decided that really didn't matter. What mattered was Robbie's current condition, which was obviously far from healthy. He was still too thin and pale, with dark circles under his bloodshot eyes. "Maybe we should send for the doctor."

Robbie shook his head as he closed his eyes. "No doctor. It's this business with Moira that has me out of sorts, that's all. I'll be fine when it's over."

"Perhaps if we went riding, or walked up the hills, that would help you sleep."

Robbie turned his head to look out the long mullioned windows. "Not today," he said with a weary sigh. "It's going to rain."

He was, unfortunately, right. The sky was a dull slate gray that foretold a downpour before the afternoon was over.

Robbie suddenly seemed to remember where Gordon had been. "So what happened?" he demanded as he squirmed to a sitting position, his feet on the floor.

"What did my former fiancée say when you told her I was suing her for breach of promise?"

Not wanting to inflame the situation even more, Gordon tried to choose his words wisely. "Naturally she was upset."

That was true, although not in the way Robbie seemed to interpret his response, judging by the gleam of triumph that came to his red-rimmed eyes. "As well she should be! Was she willing to settle out of court?"

Gordon had done his best to talk Robbie out of naming such a huge sum in damages; the best he'd been able to do was suggest that he be willing to compromise and eventually settle for a lesser amount in order to save time and expenses. After much persuading, Robbie had finally agreed. Regrettably, Lady Moira had rendered his victory moot. "No, she did not."

Robbie's expression dulled, but only for a moment. "Well then, she'll have to pay the whole amount when we win—*plus* expenses!"

Robbie had always been a confident fellow and clearly nothing that had happened to him had altered that. "She believes she will not lose."

"Ha!" Robbie snorted as he got to his feet, kicking over the bottle and paying it no heed as it rolled across the Aubusson carpet and came to a halt at the edge of the marble hearth. "Of course she will! Everybody in Dunbrachie knew we were engaged. Everybody knows she broke it off. How did you put it? Ah, yes—she breached a verbal contract. *And* I've got the best solicitor in Scotland and England, too, to represent me."

This was no time to prevaricate. "I'm flattered by

your compliments, Robbie, but she feels that given some of your less-than-exemplary behavior, a judge will be sympathetic to her."

Robbie laughed, although not with his usual merry mirth. This laugh was cold and harsh and ugly. "A female judge might take her side, but since there are no lady judges and never will be, I'll win and Moira will have to pay. And then I…"

He didn't finish as he went to what looked like a row of books, pulled one half out of its slot, and revealed another liquor cabinet.

Though Gordon didn't think Robbie should have another drink, that wasn't what bothered him most now. "And then you…what?"

"And then I'll be finished with her once and for all."

There was more to it than that, or Robbie wouldn't be suing her. He would simply leave her alone. And he'd sounded almost…desperate.

"You need the money!" Gordon blurted as an explanation for that desperation burst into his mind.

"No. That is, not exactly," Robbie said, blushing as he poured some whiskey from a Waterford decanter into a crystal glass that looked nearly as dusty as the books.

Did the man have alcohol squirreled away in every room of his house? Was that where his money was going?

But the McStuarts had been rich for generations, with more wealth than any one man could possibly drink away.

"The money would come in handy, that's all," Robbie

said as the distinct scent of whiskey reached Gordon's nostrils. "I have a few debts I'd like to get rid of sooner rather than later.

"Besides, it's the principle of the thing. She broke a contract and she ought to pay a penalty," he finished before he downed his whiskey in a gulp.

"Was that why you were going to marry her? Because her father is rich?" Gordon asked, hoping he was wrong. Silently praying that he was.

"Of course not!" Robbie retorted as he whirled around, his chest heaving with what Gordon believed— to his relief—was genuine dismay. "I loved her! You saw her—you've seen how beautiful she is. She is beautiful, isn't she?"

"Aye, very beautiful," Gordon agreed. And strong willed. And resolute. And brave and passionate and desirable.

"Who wouldn't fall in love with a woman like her? Well, maybe you wouldn't," he amended, swinging his glass around to point at Gordon and spilling a third of its contents. As with the port bottle, Robbie ignored the spill, even though the carpet had to be worth several thousand pounds. "You're far too serious and studious to fall in love, I think. Not for Gordo the insanity of Eros, eh?"

Gordon silently begged to differ. He'd been in love— or thought he was—so he knew exactly what Robbie was talking about.

"But *I* was in love," his friend continued with a dramatic flourish as, still holding the glass, he pointed to his own chest.

His declaration might have fooled somebody who didn't know Robbie well, but Gordon did, and what he saw beneath the colorful words and dramatic gestures was need. Not for Lady Moira, or her love, or even happiness, but money—and badly.

As if to prove his observation, Robbie muttered half under his breath, "It was just a bonus that her father was rich and could help me with some financial reversals I've suffered recently."

Disappointment, dismay, disgust—Gordon felt them all. And something else. Something that felt like... liberation.

Suddenly Robbie threw his glass at the hearth, shattering it into a thousand little shards. "Don't look at me like that, Gordo! Not you! It was bad enough that *she* looked at me as if I were a worm or some other loathsome creature. You're a man—aye and an attorney, too—so you should understand that sometimes men have to make rational decisions, even when it comes to marriage. *Especially* when it comes to marriage and especially if you have a title. We don't have the luxury of marrying solely for love."

There it was again—the excuse that the upper class lived by different rules. Different needs. Different choices.

Not better, Gordon noted. Just different. "I can appreciate that you take financial matters into account when you marry, Robbie." Indeed, he'd written enough marriage settlements to know that he certainly wasn't alone in that. "But what I don't understand is why a man as wealthy as you feels the need to get more money by such means."

Robbie's shoulders slumped as he let out his breath in a long sigh and sank wearily onto the sofa.

"Then I'll explain so that you can," he said, all pretence of pride or vanity gone. He was much more like the Robbie Gordon remembered as he spread his hands in a gesture of helplessness. "I'm not rich. My family hasn't been rich for years and I'm in debt up to my ears."

Gordon simply couldn't believe it. "But your family... this house... How is that possible?"

"I wasted my fair share of the family purse in my youth," Robbie admitted, "because like you and everybody else, I thought my family had plenty of money. Then my father died and I discovered he'd lost most of our family fortune gambling—cards and investments that were bound to fail. The pater clearly had no head for business and could be talked into almost anything. While my mother was alive, she managed to save him from total ruin, but after her death..." He shrugged. "My father had no one to stop him, so this estate and all our other property is mortgaged to the hilt, and we owe a fortune in other debts, too."

This wasn't the first time Gordon had heard of a family discovering that they'd been left deeply in debt. Widows especially were often shocked and dismayed to learn the extent of their husband's debts and financial obligations.

And when he considered how freely Robbie had spent

money in their youth, it became easier to believe that things could be as grim as he described.

Gordon got up and walked to the window. Out in the garden, three men were trimming a hedge. Another was weeding one of the beds.

This huge house, the town houses, the servants, Robbie's clothes, food and drink… "How are you paying for everything now?" he asked as he turned toward his friend again.

"Credit. Most of my creditors think they're the only one I've borrowed from." His elbows on his knees, he covered his face with his hands. "It's a nightmare keeping everything straight in my head because I don't dare write it down. How much I've borrowed from this one, how much from another. And when, and when they're due." He raised haunted eyes to look at Gordon. "I can't sleep, can barely eat. I'm desperate, Gordo—so desperate I've even thought of running off to America."

"Instead you decided to marry Lady Moira?"

Despite Robbie's obvious distress, it shouldn't have fallen to Lady Moira or her father or anyone else to repay the debts of the McStuarts, even if marrying for money wasn't exactly a new or innovative way for men of any class to recover from a financial loss.

His head hanging like that of a defeated general who sees his troops marching to slaughter, Robbie clasped his hands. "God, no. Not exactly, or I would have proposed to that horse-faced daughter of Lord Renfield after my father died."

He rose and came to stand in front of Gordon. "While I don't deny I was pleased Moira's dowry was considerable, that wasn't the only reason I wanted to marry her. I truly cared for her, Gordon. She's a rather remarkable woman—but stubborn and biased and too straitlaced, obviously. If only she'd been born into the title, instead of having it thrust upon her when she was already grown, she wouldn't have been so upset when she heard about those girls and we'd still be getting married and all my problems would be solved."

While Lady Moira's would be just beginning.

"There must be something else you can do," Gordon said, trying to come up with solutions that didn't involve the sacrifice of a woman's happiness.

"If there is, I'm damned if I know what it might be," Robbie replied with a shrug of his broad shoulders. "The only people who will make a loan to me now are the kind who charge exorbitant rates and hurt you if you miss a payment."

"I have some money put away that I could—" Gordon began.

"I'd rather marry an actual horse than take *your* money," Robbie interrupted. "I know how hard you work for it."

"I'm your friend, Rob, and friends help each other."

Robbie went back to the whiskey decanter and poured himself another drink. "You are helping, by representing me." He glanced sharply at Gordon as he lifted the glass. "Or are you saying you won't do that anymore?"

"No, that's not what I'm proposing," Gordon swiftly replied. Not exactly. Even though he would rather not take on such a suit as this, he wasn't going to abandon his friend. "Given that Lady Moira isn't willing to settle, this case could drag on for quite some time. We can continue the suit if you like, but surely it would be better to find another way to raise the necessary funds in a swifter fashion."

"I suppose I could propose to Lord Renfield's daughter," Robbie said with a frown after taking a sip of whiskey. "She'd accept, I'm sure, in spite of the fact that Moira jilted me." He gave Gordon a sardonic grin. "The last time her family visited here, when my father was still alive and I was a mere stripling of seventeen, I found her waiting in my bed, naked." He gave a dramatic shiver. "I've never been less tempted by a woman in my life. I covered her up in a blanket and sent her back to her room."

He owed it to Robbie as a client, as well as a friend, to give him the best advice he could. "Marrying for money is never wise. In my experience, a man or woman pays a steep price in misery and unhappiness if they do."

"Then I have no choice but to sue and hope Lady Moira's very wealthy father is forced to pay, or settle out of court for a substantial amount. I don't want to, Gordon, but…"

Robbie's gaze faltered and when he next raised his eyes, Gordon saw a vestige of the boy he'd known, or thought he had. "I'm not proud of having to resort to such measures, but what else can I do? Sir Robert McStuart can hardly advertise for a job."

"There's the law," Gordon suggested, glad he had broached the subject. "You could be a barrister."

"Are you forgetting I was never much for study? Besides, that would take more time than I have. I need money now, not years from now, or I'll have already lost the estate and town houses and what would be the point?"

Gordon surveyed the walls of the drawing room. "You could sell some of the art."

"I've borrowed against most of the good pieces," Robbie replied, "and if I were to try to sell all the rest, I might as well advertise in the *Times* that I'm bankrupt. I can just imagine what my creditors will do then."

"Perhaps I could contact your creditors on your behalf—discreetly, of course—and try to negotiate different terms for repayment or an extension. In my experience, lenders are often willing to receive something rather than nothing."

Robbie's face brightened, and he looked better than he had since Gordon had arrived. "Do you really think they'd do that?"

"It's certainly worth pursuing," Gordon assured him.

"That would be a damn sight better than asking Horse-face to marry me," Robbie said as he grinned and walked toward Gordon to shake his hand. "I swear, Gordo, inviting you here is one of the best ideas I've ever had in my life!"

Perhaps it was, but Gordon wished he'd never had it.

"Ouch!"

Sticking her index finger in her mouth before she bled on her embroidery, Moira pushed the frame away with her other hand. This was the third time she'd jabbed herself with the needle since she'd started.

She glanced at the gilded clock on the mantelpiece of the upstairs sitting room. The late-afternoon light was brighter in this part of the house if the day was sunny, so she kept all her needlework here. Today, however, had not been sunny, so there was another reason she'd chosen this relatively isolated room to spend her time.

She could see the whole long driveway from her vantage point by the window.

It was nearly time for tea, and her father still hadn't returned from Glasgow, although he should have been back by noon.

Frowning, she wrapped her handkerchief around her finger and put the small scissors, pincushion and yarns in their box, then closed the lid. This delay could mean nothing; he might have had more business to do than she suspected.

Besides, she would have to tell him about Robbie's lawsuit when he got home, and that was not something she was looking forward to. Still, the dread of telling him about that was less distressing than the dread of learning that her father had broken his vow not to imbibe to excess.

She hoped she wasn't disappointed. Again.

Sighing, she looked out the window once more, to see her father's carriage turn onto the long sweeping drive.

Chapter Five

Moira left the room at once and hurried to the top of the stairs, where she could see the foyer and watch her father enter the house.

His clothes were neat and tidy, and his gait straight and firm as he came into view.

With a relieved sigh, she rushed down the stairs and into her father's open arms.

"Moira, my girl! How I missed you!" he cried as he hugged her.

"I missed you, too, Papa," she said, holding him close, happy and relieved that he didn't smell of wine, and his eyes were clear and shining. "Your journey was a success?"

"Aye, better than I expected," he replied as he moved away to hand his coat and hat to Walters, who was waiting expectantly nearby. "I took some time to visit some of our friends, too. The Misses Jenkins all send their best, and Mrs. McGovern, and the Bruces."

"I miss them all," she said with heartfelt sincerity, taking his arm and leading him to the drawing room, where they would have their tea.

Despite her cares and duties as mistress of her father's house in Glasgow, those days often seemed like a happy, carefree dream, until his drinking had become a worry. "Perhaps we could invite Sally and her sister for a visit soon."

"Excellent idea," her father replied as he sat down before the tea table.

In addition to the tea, milk and sugar, there were scones—her father's favorite—and fresh butter and strawberry jam.

As they sat side by side on the damask-covered sofa and her father regaled her with tales of his dealings, it was almost like having tea back in their much-smaller home in Glasgow.

Almost.

"So I told the old skinflint that he should be delighted I was making such an offer," her father said with a laugh. "Just because I've got a title, I haven't lost my wits, I said. You should have seen his face, Moira!"

"Then everything went just as you'd hoped?"

"Better! That's why I was a little late returning. But I had another reason. I stand to make such a tidy profit, I stopped to get a present for a certain young lady of my acquaintance." He reached into his jacket and produced a small blue velvet box tied with a scarlet satin ribbon that he held out to her. "A trifle for my darling daughter."

Even the wrapping looked expensive. "Oh, Papa, you shouldn't have!"

"If I can't spoil my daughter, who can I spoil, at least until I have grandchildren?" he replied. "Besides, I thought you deserved something after...well, after your recent troubles."

More grateful for his sympathy, she leaned over and kissed him on the cheek.

"Enough of that! Just put it on."

She undid the ribbon and opened the box. "Oh, Papa!" she gasped at the sight of a lovely cameo of a woman's profile, the background a beautiful periwinkle blue. She lifted it out and held it up to admire against her cream-colored day gown. "It's lovely!"

"I saw it and immediately thought of you, my dear."

She pinned it to her bodice and went to look at her reflection in the mirror. It was the perfect size, and pretty and delicate.

"So, my dear, you know how my trip to Glasgow was. What have you been doing in my absence? Not spending all your time on that school, I hope."

No, she most definitely had not.

But she certainly didn't want to ruin this moment by telling him about meeting Mr. McHeath in the wood, and especially about that kiss, and surely Robbie's legal challenge could wait a little while. Too many times in recent months her time with her father had been colored by dread and dismay. "I did have a meeting with Mr. Stamford about the school."

Her father tilted his head and paused with another scone halfway to his mouth. "And?"

"And he seemed to think he could charge whatever he liked because I wouldn't be aware of the cost of building materials."

Her father chuckled before he took a bite of the scone. "More fool him. Speaking of fools, have those three idiot women done anything more to upset you?"

Moira wished her father hadn't been with her the last time she'd gone into Dunbrachie. He'd been much more disturbed by the way the three young women had given her the cut direct than she had been, in part because she didn't particularly care for the leader of the cabal, Sarah Taggart. "No, Papa, I haven't seen them lately."

He eased himself back on the sofa. "So, you've had a peaceful time in Dunbrachie, then."

Moira laced her fingers in her lap and took a deep breath. Although she would rather wait, he was going to have to hear about Robbie's lawsuit eventually, so she might as well tell him now, while he was in a good mood. And it would be better here, where all the wine and spirits were under her control. "I'm afraid there's been some difficulty with Sir Robert."

When he was sober, her father's gaze could cut like a knife. "What do you mean, difficulty?"

She swallowed hard before answering, and tried to keep her voice level and calm. "It seems, Papa, that Sir Robert has decided to sue me for breach of promise."

Her father bolted up from the sofa as if she'd stuck

him with a pin, and his face bore the same incredulous expression that had probably been on her face when McHeath had made the same announcement. *"What?"*

"Because I broke our engagement, he's suing me for breach of promise."

"That's ridiculous!" her father exclaimed, his face turning as red as ripe cherries, a stark contrast to his white hair.

"I quite agree, but ridiculous or not, that's what he's doing," she replied, her hands clasped in her lap, hoping that if she was calm, he would be, too, although it might take a while. "Apparently his attorney thinks he has a case because our engagement was public knowledge, so what can be considered a verbal contract was also public knowledge."

"Public knowledge?" her father angrily repeated. "Aye, your engagement was public knowledge and so were his liaisons with all those young women—to everybody in Dunbrachie but us!"

"Nevertheless, his solicitor said—"

"Has Gallagher lost his mind?" her father demanded, naming Sir Robert's usual solicitor, the man who'd been involved in the drafting of her marriage settlement.

"It wasn't Mr. Gallagher. The solicitor is a friend of Sir Robert's from Edinburgh, Mr. Gordon McHeath."

"I don't give a damn who he is or where he's from. They'll never win."

It was probably better to tell her father everything here and now. "Mr. McHeath said he can argue that it was my duty to find out more about Sir Robert before I accepted his proposal. Since I didn't, the fault lies with me for breaking the engagement."

Unfortunately, she had to admit, if only to herself, that Mr. McHeath was right about that one thing, at least. She should have tried to find out more about the handsome, flirtatious Sir Robert before accepting his proposal. If she hadn't been so flattered by his attention, she might have realized that he didn't stir her passion, certainly not the way Mr. McHeath did from the moment she met him.

But then, nobody had stirred her passion the way Mr. McHeath did.

Her father strode to the windows, turned and marched back again. "That man has the morals and backbone of a worm!" he declared, shaking his fist. "To sue a woman for jilting him! The man is even more of an idiot that those silly women."

"I don't think he's stupid, Papa, or that idea would never have occurred to him. He's certainly vain, though, and I've wounded his pride, enough that he's seeking five thousand pounds in compensation."

"Five thousand…?" her father gasped. "The man *is* mad if he thinks we'll pay him even a quarter of that."

"That's exactly what I told Mr. McHeath, or as good as. Perhaps once Sir Robert realizes we're not going to surrender easily, he'll drop the suit," she said as, relieved the worst of her revelations were over, she poured her father another cup of tea. "Please sit down, Papa, and have some tea."

"Tea? I can't think of tea at a time like this!" the earl cried as he stalked to the window again. He faced her once more, glowering. "You should have set the dogs on that lawyer!"

Moira didn't want to think about Mr. McHeath and dogs, and her father mustn't get so agitated. She had to find a way to calm him and deal with this problem as quickly and easily as possible, even if it was a way she didn't like.

She went to him and took his hands in hers, looking up at the man who had always striven to provide for her and make her happy despite his disturbing predilection for strong spirits in the past several months. "I've been thinking that perhaps it would be best to rid ourselves of this nuisance as swiftly as possible. It could be that if we offer Sir Robert a lesser sum, he'll leave us alone."

"Why on earth should you pay him because we found out the truth?" her father demanded, his hands gripping hers tightly. "If we hadn't and you'd married that disgraceful, dishonest rogue, he would have broken your heart and ruined your happiness."

Moira reached for the arrows in her quiver that her father would most appreciate. "Regardless of Sir Robert's behavior, my reputation is already suffering. How much more will my name be tarnished if we let this matter go to court? How much more money might we have to pay our solicitor to defend my decision?"

The earl pulled away, but not before his expression softened. "Aye, daughter, I have to admit you've got a point. If we're stubborn, it could cost us even more and not just in pounds—not that I want to pay him a cent."

"Neither do I, Papa. But it may be more prudent this

way. I'll arrange a meeting with his solicitor to test the waters."

"No, daughter. Let me deal with the rascal who's representing that blackguard."

It was on the tip of Moira's tongue to protest, until her rational mind reminded her that she was apparently unable to act in a dispassionate manner around—and with—Mr. Gordon McHeath. "Yes, Papa. More tea?"

"Checkmate," Gordon said as he moved his piece into position.

He'd suggested chess as a way to keep Robbie occupied and away from the whiskey.

He'd been partly successful, for Robbie had only had one drink during the game, leaving his empty glass sitting on the table in the library.

"Good God," Robbie muttered as he studied the chessboard. "You've obviously been playing more than I have since we last saw each other."

Given how poorly Robbie had played, Gordon could believe Robbie hadn't played at all since their last game, nearly six years ago.

Robbie slouched lower in his chair and reached for the cheroot that he'd lit a few moments ago. "I didn't realize you had such an easy life that you could play chess frequently."

"My practice consumes most of my time, but I do go out to my club a night or two a week."

"I trust you also get invited to dinner parties and such."

"Occasionally," Gordon replied, not anxious to talk

about the last dinner party he'd attended, because Catriona McNare had been in attendance, as well. Instead, he busied himself returning the chess pieces to their starting places on the board.

"Still, I envy you," Robbie said, leaning his head back and blowing out a puff of smoke. Gordon wasn't partial to the odor, so he rose and opened the nearest window.

Robbie didn't seem to notice, or else he didn't care that his smoke was bothering his friend. "Yes, I do envy you," he mused aloud. "Your quiet life. Your clear conscience."

Since meeting Moira and deciding not to tell Robbie about it, his conscience hadn't exactly been clear.

"Next time I'm thinking of getting married, Gordo, old sod, I'm going to have you to meet the gel first. A judicious, serious fellow like you will make sure I don't get jilted again."

Even if he hadn't had troubles of his own, the last thing Gordon wanted was to become Robbie's romantic consultant or vet his potential wives. "I'm no fit judge of women."

Robbie's brows rose as he sat up straighter and his eyes gleamed with interest. "If a solicitor isn't a good judge of people, who is?" He tilted his head and regarded Gordon with a studious expression, which was rare for Robert McStuart. "There's something you're not telling me, isn't there, Gordo? I can see it in the set of your jaw."

He should have been more careful. He wondered what he'd say, until Robbie solved his dilemma by speaking first. "You know all my romantic woes. It's only fair you tell me yours."

Gordon didn't want to tell Robbie about Catriona; on the other hand, it might do Robbie good to hear he wasn't the only man with romantic troubles. "There was a young lady who I thought cared for me, but I discovered I was wrong."

"Good God, Gordo!" Robbie cried, swiftly stubbing out his cheroot in his empty whiskey glass. "A woman rejected you, too? Who was she?"

"It doesn't matter. It's all over and done with, Robbie. She was already in love with another man. I wish her every happiness with her husband."

"How long has it been since she married somebody else? A month? A year?"

"A few months."

Months that had seemed like years, until he'd met Moira MacMurdaugh up in a tree.

Ever since then, he'd been realizing just how different his feelings for Catriona had been, even from the start. She had been more like a pretty doll he wanted to have in the drawing room to admire than a woman with whom he could build a life.

Moira MacMurdaugh was very much a woman, and he could easily imagine tackling life's woes as well as its joys with her by his side.

"You'll have to tell me the cure, because by God, Gordo, I've never been more wretched in my life!"

Robbie actually sounded serious.

How could he explain that the cure for a broken heart was the realization that you were never truly in love before? "Getting on with your life," he offered instead.

"Well, then, let's get started!" Robbie cried enthusiastically. "Tomorrow's market day in Dunbrachie. To be sure, it's nothing like London in the Season, or even Bath, but there's always some sort of traveling entertainers and plenty of pretty girls, too."

Gordon could foresee one possible fly in the ointment, for both of them. "Will Lady Moira be there?"

Robbie waved his hand dismissively. "I don't give a damn if she is, and neither should you. Besides, she'll steer clear of us if she is, I'm sure. Come on, Gordo! Say you'll go!"

They probably shouldn't. Robbie might get drunk, or try to seduce a barmaid or some other woman. He might do something else that would be embarrassing. And he really didn't want to see Lady Moira again. She was making his life so…complicated.

On the other hand, she might not be there, and raising Robbie's spirits might be one way to convince him to drop the suit. "All right, Robbie. I'll go."

Chapter Six

Dressed in a gown of green-and-blue-stripped muslin, with a blue velvet Spencer jacket and straw bonnet with matching ribbon on her head, her reticule slung over her arm and wearing her second-best kid gloves, Moira strolled down the main street of Dunbrachie toward the green. At one end of the street was the church, with its square belfry. At the other was the tavern and livery stable.

Between the church and tavern were several stone buildings whitewashed or not, with slate roofs and smoke curling from their chimneys. She passed the baker's and the bookseller's, separated by a narrow lane leading to yards in the back, the milliner's, the tea shop and the candle maker's.

Since it was market day, temporary stalls surrounded the green. Some were no more than the open back of a wagon and some, belonging to traveling peddlers, were more elaborate.

It was pleasantly warm and sunny, and the delicious scent of bread and pastries from the baker's drifted on the breeze. Small children and dogs chased each other around the stalls, or stood and watched the puppet show that had been set up near the middle of the green.

None of the dogs she could see were as big or as black or as ugly and vicious as the one that had chased her up the tree.

Perhaps that had been a stray or a wild dog, abandoned or lost by its owner.

Indeed, today Dunbrachie was like a rustic idyll, far removed from the teeming, bustling, aggressive market in Glasgow where she'd shopped before her father had become prosperous enough to have food and other goods delivered to their home. In some ways, she missed that market, for there she would be relatively anonymous except to those merchants whose stalls she frequented.

In Dunbrachie, everybody knew who she was, as well as the story of her father's unforeseen inheritance and her broken engagement to Sir Robert McStuart. Here she was subject to more than the glares of angry men who saw her school as a threat; there were the furtive looks, the scandalized whispers, the knowing glances and scornfully curled lips of the women, epitomized by the three young women she thought of as the Three Geese.

It might have been easier to stay at home, except

that she had no intention of allowing gossip and rude behavior make her a prisoner in her own home.

Nor was she going to be intimidated by the glares of the men who didn't want her to build her school, most notably Big Jack MacKracken, who stood six feet tall in his bare feet. At the moment he was among the several men gathered at the tavern, where benches and tables had been set outside on such a fine day. If looks could wound, his glower would have had her writhing on the ground.

However, his angry gaze couldn't hurt her, so lifting her head high, she marched past, heading for the wagon belonging to Sam Corlett, which was bedecked with ribbons, feathers, laces and trims as if it were a huge hat.

A shadow crossed her path. A broad-shouldered shadow.

"What do ye think yer about, anyway?" Big Jack demanded.

Obviously, he was no longer at the tavern. Just as obviously, judging by the odor of ale emanating from him, he'd been drinking for some time.

She wasn't afraid of him. They were in too public a place for him to do her any real harm, and now there was her title to offer additional protection. A man like MacKracken would appreciate that his punishment would be severe if he physically attacked a lady.

She gave him the same cold look she gave to merchants who tried to cheat her. "My purpose here is none of your business, Mr. MacKracken."

"Mister, is it? Think you can sweet-talk me, do you,

with yer 'misters'? Not likely—any more than any of my bairns'll ever set foot in that school you're building."

He had seven children, the oldest a girl of eleven, and all of them could benefit if they went to school. "Education is something to be cherished, Mr.—"

"If ye wants yer children growin' up wantin' things they can ne'er have," he retorted. "What good is readin' and writin' to a man does a man's work on a farm? Aye, or his wife?"

"None, perhaps," she replied, keeping her voice level, "unless they have to sign a bill of sale, or a will, or some other legal document. And who's to say your boys will want to be laborers? My father was born poor and yet he's achieved great success, which he wouldn't have been able to do if he hadn't learned to read and write."

"He got a title because some cousin he ne'er even met died."

"He was successful in business long before that."

And before he'd started drinking too much. Mercifully his drinking had been confined to overimbibing at night, at first rarely, but in the last few months, more frequently. However, he had never stayed drunk for days in a row, for which she was grateful, and that meant his business hadn't suffered. Yet.

MacKracken scowled. "So you say, m'lady."

"Aye, so I do," she replied. "Now if you'll excuse me, I have some purchases to make."

She started forward without waiting for the big man to move. Fortunately, he did, or she didn't know what she would have done. She couldn't count on Mr. McHeath coming to her rescue again, even if he were here.

She had already ascertained, by a swift perusal of the green, that he was not.

She joined a group of older girls and women already gathered at Sam Corlett's wagon. If they had witnessed her encounter with MacKracken, they gave no sign, although none ventured more than a greeting and a curtsey, and all kept a careful distance from her.

"Good day, my lady!" Sam cried in his Cockney accent when he spotted her, tugging his forelock and grinning, for she'd bought from him before. "I was hopin' you'd be here today. Got some lovely bits o' ribbon today. Perfect for a lady like yourself."

"I need some green ribbon, Sam. Light green."

His eyes lit up like a candle in the dark. "As a matter o' fact, my lady, I've got just the thing!"

He reached into the back of his wagon, moving some cotton thread and what looked like dyed goose feathers out of the way before producing a bolt of apple-green grosgrain that was exactly what she required.

But betray too eager a countenance she would not. "How much?"

"Tuppence a yard."

Ah, Sam, she thought with pleasant respect. Always trying to get the better of her in a bargain—as well he should. Nevertheless, he had named a price at least twice what the ribbon was worth, and probably four times what he'd paid for it.

Happily playing the game, she kept her expression

grave as she raised an inquiring brow. "Is it from France?"

His visage assumed an equally grave, somewhat dismayed, appearance. "No, miss, no. Good British ribbon, that is."

Both her brows rose. "Really? I thought it must be foreign for you to charge such an outrageous price."

"Well, now, my lady, there's transport involved, that's for certain, feed costin' what it does these days. And the effort to find the best, o' course. I don't just buys any ribbon, as you know. That's the best to be had in Scotland at any price."

"I don't need the *best,* Sam," she countered.

"I have this, then," he said, reaching into his wagon and pulling out a roll of a green ribbon of a shade that surely didn't exist in nature, or anywhere else except a dyer's, if the dyer had terrible eyesight.

"That's quite an interesting color, but this one will match better," she said. "Still, at tuppence a yard, it's too dear for what I intend."

She turned away as if planning to leave.

"I suppose, since you're such a pretty lady, I could let you have two yards for a tuppence," Sam suggested.

Keeping any triumph from her expression, she turned back. "Really? Oh, that would be wonderful," she said, giving him a smile. "It *is* lovely ribbon."

Sam's answering grin told her she was paying exactly the amount he wanted and had expected, satisfying them both.

"Listen to her haggling like a fishwife, and her father

rich as Croesus!" a peevish feminine voice muttered nearby.

Miss Sarah Taggart. And no doubt her two acolytes were with her.

Miss Sarah Taggart, an ironmonger's daughter, Miss Mabel Hornby, sister of the local miller, and Miss Emmeline Swanson, niece of a prominent distiller, had been keen to be Moira's friends when she'd first arrived in Dunbrachie. Once Robbie started to pay more attention to her than to them, however, and especially once she was engaged to him, their attitude had turned frosty.

After the engagement had been broken, she'd wondered if they'd try to befriend her again. They had not, choosing instead to cut her.

Or rather, Miss Sarah Taggart had chosen to cut her, and therefore so did her comrades.

However, she had no intention of giving Sarah the satisfaction of letting her know she'd heard her.

Instead, she paid Sam and, with her ribbon, started back toward the livery stable. Her steps slowed as she drew near the baker's. Baked goods were plentiful at home, so she had no need to purchase anything; it was just the wonderful rich smell of fresh bread and pastries that made her linger until she heard two familiar male voices, one jovial and jesting, the other more sedate.

Sir Robert McStuart and Mr. Gordon McHeath— two people she wanted to meet even less than Big Jack MacKracken and Sarah Taggart.

Trying to look as if she were doing nothing out of the ordinary, she darted into the narrow lane between the baker's and the bookshop before Robbie and McHeath walked past.

Although her instinct told her to avoid them both, she couldn't resist looking at McHeath as he passed.

This morning he didn't look at all like a solicitor. He wore a comfortable-looking wool jacket and trousers, with a plain vest and loosely knotted cravat, his tall hat shoved back on his head, revealing his thick waving hair. Dressed thus, it was far easier to see him as the man who had come to her aid instead of the solicitor representing the man for whom she'd lost all respect and whom she could never love.

However, he was that solicitor, and it occurred to her that if they were going to offer to settle, it might be best to start negotiations as soon as possible, without her father.

Even if that meant risking being alone with Mr. McHeath.

Seeing the way the villagers of Dunbrachie reacted to Robbie's presence, Gordon could understand the origin of his friend's arrogance. People smiled and nodded and tugged their forelock as he passed. Men moved out of his way as if he were a conquering hero, and women of all ages blushed if he so much as glanced their way. Small children stared in openmouthed awe and older boys with envy. Older girls giggled and looked modestly at their feet. Even the dogs seemed to regard him with deference—and Gordon duly noted that none of the dogs were huge and black.

Robbie seemed to accept the attention of the crowd as

his due, reacting with the same sort of noblesse oblige he'd displayed toward Gordon when they were boys at school. Then Gordon had felt as if he'd been the chosen of the gods, and he hadn't experienced anything quite so thrilling since.

Except once, when Lady Moira had kissed him.

He had to stop thinking about that, just as he ought to stop looking for her here. After all, why would she come to a village market? Merchants and tradesmen would be only too delighted to bring anything she might need or want to purchase to her father's manor house.

"Oh, God, go left. To your left!" Robbie muttered under his breath, shoving Gordon in that direction with his elbow as they neared a wagon decorated like it was part of a May Day celebration imagined by a madman.

"Why? What's wrong?" Gordon asked in a whisper, although he could think of only one possibility, and it was one that made his heart race, although he shouldn't be excited by the possibility of another confrontation with Lady Moira.

Especially when he was with Robbie.

A swift glance over his shoulder brought a disappointment equal to his previous enthusiasm, for instead of Lady Moira, three young women dressed in what was probably the height of fashion in Dunbrachie were bustling toward them. The young woman in the lead was tall, bright-eyed and auburn haired, and possessed a wide smile that revealed slightly crooked teeth. Her pelisse was light blue, and her bonnet was decorated with flowers and ribbon to match. Trailing her like faithful handmaidens were a shorter, blonde, slightly plump young woman in a pelisse with frog closings and a smaller bonnet, as well as another dark-haired companion, who was dressed in a green gown, dark green Spencer jacket and a very wide-brimmed, overembellished hat.

Wondering how he and Robbie could escape, for that seemed the best thing to do, he turned toward his friend.

Who was no longer beside him.

Halting in confusion, Gordon spotted Robbie disappearing through the door of the tavern. *He* hadn't gone left; he'd made a sharp right turn, obviously deciding to abandon his friend to his fate, or at least the three young women.

"I beg your pardon for being so bold," the tall, auburn-haired young woman said as she stopped and curtsied, "but you *are* Mr. McHeath, aren't you? Sir Robert's friend from Edinburgh? I would ask him for an introduction, but he's not here and my friends and I—this is Miss Mabel Hornby and Miss Emmeline Swanson—have been most anxious to make your acquaintance. I hope you don't mind."

Trapped, Gordon nevertheless bowed and answered politely. "Yes, I'm Gordon McHeath, from Edinburgh. I'm delighted to make your acquaintance."

The Misses Hornby and Swanson giggled, while the spokeswoman went happily on. "I'm Sarah Taggart—Miss Sarah Taggart. We don't often have visitors from Edinburgh in Dunbrachie. That is, Sir Robert has visitors, but they don't often come to the village."

"It's their loss, I'm sure."

"It's so good of you to come to cheer Sir Robert up during this time of trial," Miss Taggart continued in a mournful tone, although her eyes remained bright and alert, as if she were some sort of predatory bird. "We think he's been very badly used."

"Very badly," Miss Swanson breathlessly seconded, while Miss Hornby nodded so rapidly, her extravagantly decorated hat looked in immediate danger of falling off her head. The very wide, brilliantly green ribbons were doing their job of keeping it in place, although it also looked as if the huge bow was keeping her head on her neck, as well.

"That wouldn't have happened if he'd chosen a local girl," Miss Taggart declared.

Her friends nodded enthusiastically. No doubt they were local girls, and he wondered vaguely how long their friendships would last if Robbie were to choose one of them.

"There are several suitable young women in and around Dunbrachie who would be honored to be his bride."

"Honored!" she of the precarious bonnet echoed.

"Delighted!" cried the other young lady.

Miss Taggart glanced at her companions before continuing. "Please let him know that he has friends in the village who think what's happened to him is a terrible shame—but what else can you expect from strangers? And from Glasgow, too!"

She said "Glasgow" as if that city was a modern

Gomorrah and anybody from that location should be automatically discounted as worthy of matrimony.

"I'm sure he already knows he has friends in Dunbrachie," Gordon replied, wondering if these women would be so enthusiastically sympathetic if they knew Robbie had just purposefully avoided them.

Or how much he drank. And his debts. And the number of women he'd seduced.

Or maybe they already did and didn't care, because Robbie was titled and handsome. As for the lawsuit, they might think that justified, too, not realizing, as Gordon unfortunately had, that it indicated a level of bitter vindictiveness no man of honor and true nobility should possess. "Now if you'll excuse me, I have some business to attend to."

Such as keeping Robbie from drinking himself into a stupor in the tavern.

"Oh, yes, of course. Good day, Mr. McHeath," Miss Taggart said with another grimacelike smile before she took the arm of each of her friends and sauntered off as if she had just made a romantic conquest.

Nothing could be further from the truth, Gordon thought as he started toward the tavern, passing the lane between the baker's and a bookshop. The next time he and Robbie were in a similar situation, should there be a similar situation—

A hand reached out, grabbed his shoulder and pulled him backward into the lane.

Chapter Seven

Gordon raised his hand to strike—until he realized his assailant was wearing a bonnet.

A *woman* had pulled him into the alley—a woman wearing a bonnet as prettily and expensively decorated as anything Lady Catriona McNare had ever worn, covering glossy dark hair. Her Spencer jacket was velvet, her gown of fine muslin....

He knew who it was even before the bonnet tilted back to reveal Lady Moira's face. "My lady, what—?"

She put her fingers to his lips to silence him. Although she wore gloves, her light touch was as arousing as a caress along his naked thigh. "Please, speak quietly, Mr. McHeath," she whispered. "If I'm going to be humble and eat a little crow, I prefer to do it with as few witnesses as possible."

He would have obeyed any order she gave when she looked at him like that and touched his mouth.

"I have decided that I should, perhaps, be more flexible in my dealings with Sir Robert."

Why did she have to mention Robbie?

"I'm prepared to consider settling out of court, to save all of us time and expense."

Of course. It was the lawsuit that brought them together, and the lawsuit, as well as his friendship with Robbie, would keep them apart, always.

Yet he should be glad about this latest development, and not just for Robbie's sake. His life was in Edinburgh, not here. She was a lady; he was a lawyer. Her family was rich, her father an earl; he had no family at all, or none to speak of. His parents had died when he was a clerk and no siblings had survived infancy. All his aunts or uncles were dead, and his only surviving cousin had emigrated to Canada.

Determined to remember the differences that must keep them apart, he forced himself to think and speak like the solicitor he was. "How much are you willing to offer to settle the suit?"

"What do you think Robbie will be willing to accept?"

He had learned long ago that women could be as clever or good at negotiating as men, having dealt with many wives and widows of merchants who were just as canny as their husbands when it came to business transactions, and some much more so.

Although he was well aware he had to think clearly and carefully during any negotiation, none of the other women he'd bargained with or represented had been as intriguing or interesting as Lady Moira, and he had

certainly never kissed any of them, circumstances that
were making it extremely difficult for him to keep his
focus strictly on the business at hand.

He was also well aware that it would be to his advantage to try to get her to make the first suggestion as to
an amount. "Ladies first, as they say."

"I suppose I should make it clear that while I'm willing to discuss a settlement, I make no admission of guilt
or misconduct on my part. As for any emotional distress,
I'm *quite* sure I didn't break Robbie's heart, so any offer
I make is done with the sole intention of ridding my life
of him once and for all."

She spoke in such a calm and cool manner, he could
well believe she had forgotten their kiss. Or—almost
worse—that it had not been the mind-shattering, heart-
stopping experience for her that it had been for him.

"You sound very certain of my friend's feelings, or
lack of them," he noted. "You can't see into a man's
heart, can you?"

Or what would she see in his?

"You can't see into his heart, either," she returned.
"I realize you're his friend, but as a lawyer, you must
also be aware that people lie."

She tilted her head to study him, and he had the
uncomfortable feeling that she understood him, and all
men, too well. "If he ever truly loved me, why does he
want to hurt me now? Why not simply let us go our
separate ways? After all, his reputation will recover
much sooner than mine."

She was right, and yet he had a job to do, whether
he wanted to or not. He had told Robbie he'd represent

him, so represent him he must. "Do you not consider that his anger could be proof of his pain? If he cared less, it would be easier for him to let the matter drop."

She was clearly not at all convinced by his argument. "Then what about his actions after I told him I couldn't and wouldn't marry him? I have it on good authority that he was with another woman that very same night."

Unfortunately, Gordon could easily believe that Robbie had indeed sought either comfort or oblivion in the arms of a woman as soon as possible. Nevertheless, if he'd done so that same night, Robbie should have told him that, because she was right to think it would make his case weaker.

"So, he's not been completely honest with you, either," she observed.

Somewhere between Edinburgh and Dunbrachie he'd obviously lost the ability to maintain an attorney's dispassionate mask, at least when speaking to Lady Moira MacMurdaugh.

He also seemed to be taking everything Lady Moira said at face value, which he really ought not to do. She did, after all, have a reason to discredit his friend. "How do you know this?"

"My father had it from the innkeeper where Sir Robert met the woman."

"In other words," he began, determined to do his best for Robbie as well as remain as cool and composed as she and reveal nothing more of his feelings, "your source is gossip."

"Do you really think my father would have told me that if it wasn't true?"

"I have no idea what your father might say," Gordon replied, "and he is hardly in a neutral position. As for whether or not I was informed of Sir Robert's activities on the night in question, if a man seeks solace with a woman, he need not confide that to a friend, or his lawyer, or anyone. Nor does that mean his pain is any the less."

"Nevertheless it suggests that he was consolable, and if so, the pain of our broken engagement was not so severe that he should receive five thousand pounds in reparation. I would think five hundred would be more than sufficient," she finished, her eyes shining with what looked like a combination of delight and excitement, as if this was some sort of competition she was determined to win. In a way, of course, it was—but while he'd seen that reaction from some lawyers and merchants in similar circumstances, he'd never encountered it in a woman before.

Another example, should he require one, of what made this particular woman so different. And so fascinating.

And why he had to fight to keep his mind on the business at hand, as well as remembering he represented Robbie, not her.

"There is also the matter of his wounded pride," he pointed out. "He may think settling for such a small sum is another wound."

"I agree Robbie has a great deal of pride—much more than he deserves, so I don't intend to reward him for it."

"Whether you think his pride is justified or not, it

is something that must be taken into account. He is a titled man, after all. I doubt he'll settle for less than four thousand."

"Perhaps he should remember his pride and his title the next time he starts drinking," she countered.

Gordon couldn't disagree, so he turned the subject back to the financial. "If you offer too small a sum, he may consider that as much of an insult as breaking your engagement," he warned.

"I will not pay more than eight hundred pounds, and I consider that a gift."

Robbie would surely consider that a pittance, take umbrage, lose his temper and drink even more. "Eight hundred pounds will surely not be enough. Indeed, it may make him think you aren't taking this suit seriously."

"I assure you, I do. It's Sir Robert I don't take seriously."

"You should, my lady. He's very determined in this matter. I think you should offer at least three thousand."

"I am determined, too, Mr. McHeath—determined that he won't get more than a thousand pounds, and that's a thousand pounds more than he should. He should be delighted I'm willing to consider paying him anything at all."

"My lady, I fear that won't be enough to satisfy him."

He saw the change come over her, and knew that she would go no higher even before she said, "We have haggled enough, Mr. McHeath. If he'd rather take this case to court than be reasonable and grateful for my offer, so be it. Good day."

Whether he represented Robbie or not, he couldn't let her go, not like that, so as she turned to leave the lane, he put a detaining hand on her arm. "Lady Moira, I appreciate your willingness to compromise and perhaps I'm wrong to say what Sir Robert will or will not accept. I'll take your offer to him and inform you of the outcome."

He couldn't help it. He had to tell her how he really felt about the suit. "I regret my friend's action in this matter, but I owe him too much to refuse to represent him."

Her steadfast gaze held him as if there was a web binding them together. "What do you owe him?" she asked softly.

He wanted her to know. He needed her to know, to understand. "My reputation. My education. My career. When we were at school together, I stole some money to buy sweets. Not much, but it would have seen me disgraced and expelled. Robbie told the headmaster he did it. If he hadn't, I would have had to go to a less prestigious school, wouldn't have gotten the job clerking for as fine and reputable solicitor as I did, and likely wouldn't be a solicitor myself. That is what I owe Robbie—certainly far too much to turn my back on him now, even though he's…changed."

She took hold of the lapels of Gordon's jacket as if he was falling away from her, and her increasingly intense scrutiny seemed to bore into his soul. "Even if he helped you years ago, how can you represent him now? He's a cad who seduces and abandons vulnerable young women."

"Robbie's been raised to believe that, as a nobleman, it is his right."

"It's not!"

"No, it isn't," he agreed. "He should have resisted temptation."

As he should be resisting temptation now. As he must, even though he gently cupped her shoulders. "You should go, Lady Moira," he said softly.

Lady Moira nodded, but she didn't move. Her whole body flushed with warmth beneath his steadfast, yearning gaze.

"Or I should go," he murmured. "*Somebody* should go before…"

"Yes, before…" she whispered as he drew her into his arms.

This was a mistake, Moira told herself as he put his arms around her. In spite of the passion smoldering in his eyes and the heat of her own longing, despite the memory of his lips against hers and masculine strength of his body, she should push him away and flee.

She didn't. She couldn't.

She stepped closer, yielding to her desire as she raised herself on her toes and lifted her face for his kiss. Her fingers stopped clutching the cloth of his jacket to lie flat against his rapidly rising and falling chest.

This time, it was no gentle, seeking, tender brushing of lips. The moment their mouths met, it was as if they were torches bursting into flame, to be consumed completely.

With a low moan of surrender, she wrapped her arms around him and pressed her body against his. She forgot everything and everybody, where she was, who he was. She was aware only of the need to be in this man's arms, to taste his kiss and feel the caress of his hands.

And caress her he did with his free hand as, with the other arm around her, he guided her back until she was against the wall of the bakery. While his tongue thrust into her open and willing mouth, he stroked her cheek, her shoulder, her arm. Her ribs and, finally, her breast.

She groaned at the pleasure his touch aroused, the sound muffled by his mouth. He braced himself with his left hand against the wall, and his right hand continued to entice her to new heights of need, his lips and tongue promising yet more excitement.

She, too, stroked and caressed, her passionate fervor growing as she ran her hands over the powerful muscles of his arms and back and shoulders. Emboldened by the craving rushing through her, she slipped her hand inside his vest to feel the heat of his skin through his linen shirt.

One of the shirt buttons gave way, and she instinctively slid her hand inside to glide over his naked chest, the hairs around his nipple coarse compared to the silk of his skin.

With greater urgency he angled himself closer, his knee sliding between hers, the hardness of his limb at the junction of her thighs increasing the already-ardent demand within her.

His lips slipped from her mouth, moving down the throbbing pulse of her neck. Panting, she arched and pushed her body against his thigh. His hand went to her breast again, kneading, as his mouth glided toward her collarbone and the edge of her bodice.

He tugged her forward against his half-raised thigh, pushing and almost instantly releasing. She had no idea why he did that, only that she didn't want him to stop. The pressure was too exhilarating, while a tension of a sort she had never experienced before began to build.

He cradled her breast with his free hand, whisking the pad of his thumb across the tip of her bodice where her nipple pebbled beneath the fabric. Again he pulled her forward against the hard strength of his thigh. Then she pushed against him herself, over and over, as the thrilling, breathtaking tension built and built.

Then the tension shattered, like a pane of brittle glass. He muffled her cries of release by covering her mouth with his, in another searing kiss.

She had no words, no real thoughts beyond amazement, too shocked and benumbed by what had just happened to utter a sound.

Chapter Eight

As Moira stared at Gordon, her face flushed, her eyes wide with dazed incredulity, guilt overwhelmed his unsatisfied need.

What had he done?

How could he have been so weak? Shown so little judgment?

He should not have given in to the impulses that coursed through him whenever he was with her, especially when he was helping Robbie to sue her.

"Moira," he began, although he had no idea what he was going to say, whether to try to explain, or apologize.

Her expression changed to one of stark horror, as if he'd tried to murder her. She shook her head and held up her hand to ward him off. "No," she whispered, "no, no, no! I've never…not with anyone…!"

She'd never and not with anyone…what? She'd

never been so intimate with a man, a thought that both thrilled and relieved him, or been so weak, a dismay he shared?

Before he could ask, before he could try to explain or attempt to excuse his actions—although there could be no real explanation beyond pure, unadulterated desire, of a sort he hadn't felt since...of a sort he had *never* felt—she pushed her way past him and ran out of the lane.

He started to follow her, then stopped. What could he possibly say that would make him sound any better than Robbie, a man she had jilted for lack of self-control?

As he slumped back against the wall, one thing above all else was clear in his mind. Whatever was happening between him and Lady Moira, he couldn't stay in Dunbrachie, not even for Robbie. He would give Robbie the work he'd already done, wish him good luck with a new solicitor and return to Edinburgh. Robbie would be angry, perhaps angry enough to never see or speak to him again, but would that be any worse than finding himself at the mercy of a passion he couldn't control?

He had to get back to Edinburgh, to familiar surroundings and what would feel like solid ground instead of this rocky, unstable terrain. To be sure, his heart had been wounded in Edinburgh, but at least that was familiar, too.

He also couldn't stay in this lane forever.

Determined to find Robbie and go back to McStuart House, but equally determined that no one know he'd been near Lady Moira, let alone talked to her, let alone kissed her, he left the lane at the opposite end. He strode across the green and shoved open the door to the tavern, a rather run-down establishment of gray granite and slate, with a huge hearth that smoked, and several patrons who did, too, so that the air of the taproom was redolent of smoke, tobacco, sweat, sawdust and ale. It was noisy, too, from the voices of several men, including Robbie's.

As his eyes grew accustomed to the sudden dimness, he searched for his friend and saw him at the far end of the room. Robbie was sprawled in a chair, a wine bottle on the table in front of him and several men who looked like merchants or tradesmen around him, listening to him as if intent on his every word.

On the opposite side near the door of the low-ceilinged room was another group of what looked like farmers or laborers. They, too, had someone occupying the center of attention—a tall, beefy fellow dressed in rough homespun, who looked as if he washed no more than once a year.

"I took her down a peg or two," the unwashed man crowed in triumph as Gordon entered.

He was probably talking about his no doubt down-trodden wife.

"Thinks she's so high-and-mighty, with her money and her title, tellin' us all what's best for our children. I told her what she could do with her bloody school."

Gordon's steps slowed and his resolve to leave immediately lessened a little. How many titled women could there be in Dunbrachie?

"She had the gall to cast her pa up to me. He made money before he inherited the title, says she, because he can read and write. So what if he can? He was born lucky if ever a man was. Well, most of us ain't!"

The men around him nodded. "That's right, Jack," one of them, a short man with a squint, agreed.

"Gordo, old chap, here you are!" Robbie called out, and Gordon had no choice but to approach him.

As he got closer to Robbie's table, he got a better look at the men he was with. They looked like the sort of hail-fellow-well-met rascals that Robbie would find entertaining and be happy to entertain, the same sort who could easily goad him into paying for every round of drinks and gamble with him until he had nothing left in his wallet.

Gordon joined them, but he did not sit down, and he only made the most perfunctory nod as he was introduced to men he'd likely never meet again. "Gentlemen," he said to them all. "Sir Robert, if you don't mind, I think it's time we returned to McStuart House."

"It's not even noon!" Robbie protested with frowning dismay.

"Rather past it," Gordon replied. Robbie had already finished a bottle of wine, by the looks of it, and by himself, for the other men all had mugs of ale either in their hands or on the table in front of them.

Robbie ignored him and addressed the men at the table.

"Well, what did I tell you, boys?" He pushed back his chair, jumped to his feet and threw his arm companionably around Gordon's shoulder. "Built like a first-class prizefighter, isn't he? He was the champion of the school when we were boys."

That was true and once he would have been thrilled to hear Robbie boasting of his prowess, but not now. It wasn't an accomplishment he was particularly proud of, and he wanted to go. "Sir Robert—"

"I don't know what you do in Edinburgh to stay so healthy, Gordo," Robbie interrupted with a laugh, "but clearly, it's working."

It was on the tip of Gordon's tongue to say that one thing he didn't do was drink to excess; however, such a comment would likely only drive Robbie to insist upon staying, and drinking more. "If you don't mind, Sir Robert," he said with more firmness, "I'd like to go back to McStuart House."

Again Robbie ignored him. "I'll wager fifty pounds Gordon here can beat anybody you bring against him."

Oh, God! Gordon opened his mouth to protest, but before he could, one of the men, wearing a particularly bright yellow vest, cried, "I'll take that bet."

He rose and slapped a purse of coins on the table.

He was pale and his hands were too soft to indicate he worked for a living. He might be a nobleman or well-to-do merchant or tradesman, yet there was something about his clothes—the quality of the cloth, the vulgar bright yellow of his waistcoat—that suggested he was more likely a professional gamester.

Which made it all the more imperative that he get Robbie out of there. Otherwise, who could say how much more Robbie would spend that he didn't have, or what other mischief he might get into.

"I haven't boxed since we left school and I have no

intention of boxing today," Gordon said, determined to leave the tavern with his friend as quickly as possible.

"Oh, don't be an old woman!" Robbie chided, his grin a little forced, the look in his eyes a little hard. "You can surely beat anybody from around here with one hand tied behind your back."

"I've already taken the bet," the gamester reminded them, his eyes gleaming with triumphant greed.

"I didn't agree," Gordon returned.

"A bet's a bet," the gamester insisted. "Ain't that right, boys? Unless you ain't blokes what keeps their word."

"I've never gone back on a bet in my life," Robbie declared, taking hold of Gordon's arm with a fierce grip. "Just give me a few moments to help my friend get over his reluctance."

Gordon didn't appreciate being treated like a recalcitrant child; nevertheless, it would probably only makes things worse if he refused to go with Robbie, so he allowed Robbie to lead him through the bustling kitchen. A buxom, plump woman whose hair was covered with a kerchief and whose apron bore traces of many a spill stirred a pot of what smelled like beef stew. She stared openmouthed as they passed, revealing a few remaining teeth. A scullery maid who looked as if she hadn't eaten a decent meal in weeks stood at the stone sink, a dirty pot and equally dirty rag in her hands. Although she was clearly just as surprised as the other woman and her eyes were on Robbie and Gordon, she mechanically kept swishing the rag in the pot. A lad of about ten with a load of kindling in his hands dropped it, shocking the woman at the pot back into motion, and the scullery maid picked up another pot.

Paying absolutely no attention to them, kicking a basket of turnips out of the way, Robbie proceeded to the yard, Gordon in tow.

Once out into the fresh air and bright sunlight, Gordon blinked like a mole and surveyed the yard bordered by a rugged stone fence on two sides and what appeared to be a stable on the third. A covered well was near the door, and so were several empty casks and barrels. A wooden trough rested against one of the walls and a few chickens scratched in the dirt.

Otherwise, they were alone.

Good.

"I'm not going to fight anybody," Gordon told Robbie firmly as he faced him. "I'm a twenty-eight-year-old solicitor, not a schoolboy."

Anxious to win your respect and admiration.

Robbie folded his arms over his chest. "What harm will it do?" he demanded, his words slightly slurred. "Your reputation won't be sullied. This isn't Edinburgh, after all. And who do you think they'll bring against you? Some young yokel who's likely never boxed before, I'll wager. It'll be easy money."

For Robbie, but it would be Gordon doing the fighting.

It was bad enough that Robbie was trying to claw his way out of debt by suing Lady Moira, but now he wanted to use him to win a wager, as well? "I don't want to fight, Robbie."

His face reddening, Robbie crossed his arms over his

chest and glared at Gordon. "I never thought you'd turn coward on me."

Gordon's ire rose and whatever respect he'd retained for Robbie vanished. "I'm not afraid to fight. I don't *want* to fight today, whether you've made a wager—"

An idea came to him, a way to make Robbie give up the suit, and since Robbie so obviously liked to gamble, surely it would appeal to him. "I'll fight on one condition, Robbie. If I win, you agree to…"

He hesitated. He wanted to say that if he won, Robbie had to drop the suit completely, except that Robbie would probably never agree to that. So instead, he went for an option Robbie would likely at least be willing to consider. "If I win, you agree to settle the suit with Lady Moira for one thousand pounds and we find another way to get you out of the rest of your debts, or at least make them manageable."

Robbie frowned as he leaned his weight on one leg. "Why should I agree to that?"

Gordon didn't want to risk losing this chance, so he came up with a reason a man like Robbie could appreciate. "Because this way, the suit will be settled easier and quicker, and you'll have some money sooner. That amount should enable you to keep your most pressing creditors at bay for a little while, at least."

"And less work for you, too, eh, Gordo?" Robbie noted with a smirk.

A few days ago, Gordon would have said he could never hate Robbie McStuart, but standing in the yard of the tavern in Dunbrachie, seeing that smirk after learning what his friend had done and what he was capable of, the last vestige of respect, affection and admiration he had for Sir Robert McStuart dwindled away.

"What if you fight and lose?" Robbie asked.

"I'll pay the wager."

"And the suit? You won't try to make me settle for less than five thousand?"

"I won't try to make you do anything, because I won't be representing you in that anymore, regardless of the outcome of the fight."

Robbie stared at him incredulously. "What?"

"You heard me, Robbie. If you want to continue your suit against Lady Moira, you'll have to find another solicitor. I'll leave you the documents I've drafted."

He'd also leave a sealed letter for the new solicitor suggesting that Lady Moira might be willing to offer a settlement for a lesser amount, leaving it to the new solicitor to negotiate the exact terms. "I'm going back to Edinburgh as soon as possible."

"By God, you really mean it!" Robbie cried incredulously.

"Yes, Robbie, I really do. I think that lawsuit is a mistake."

Instead of being angry, Robbie threw back his head and laughed, as if everything was all right between them, although it never would be again. "Good God, Gordo! I knew you had a bit of the Calvinist in you, but I had no idea it ran so deep. Sweet Jesus, you almost make me ashamed of myself."

Almost, but not truly ashamed, as he ought to be. As any truly honorable gentleman would be.

"There's no need to go rushing back to Edinburgh,

old friend, because you're going to win the fight, and when you do, I'll settle for a thousand pounds and as long as you'll help me deal with those creditors, all will be well with the world."

Gordon marvelled at the ease with which Robbie dismissed opposition. He had always been carefree in their youth, but Gordon had assumed it was because he was rich and titled. Now that ability took on a more selfish quality. It was as if Robbie simply assumed and accepted as his right that his troubles would always be solved somehow, by someone else.

Thank God, Lady Moira had broken their engagement. Marriage to a man like Robbie would be a misery.

"Come on, Gordo, no more time to waste. They'll have the ring set up by now. We'll have to find you something else to wear, though. I wouldn't want you to ruin your clothes."

As if his clothes were all he should be worried about.

After Moira left the lane, she wanted nothing more than to get to her carriage and back home as quickly as possible. She hurried along the street past the shops and houses, head down, eyes on the uneven pavement, not wanting to stop, or be stopped by anyone, making every effort not to glance over her shoulder to see if McHeath had followed her out of the lane. Or where he was at all.

How could she have been so foolish? So weak? So stupid? To let him kiss her again… To surrender to the desire he aroused. To be so bold and wanton, brazen and reckless. To let him stroke and caress her, until…

"Good morning, my lady."

She came to a halt and turned toward eleven-year-old Lillibet MacKracken, who was dressed in a much-mended calico dress, bareheaded, her face tanned, and ankles skinny above boots too large for her feet. The little girl grinned shyly at her from the edge of the milliner's shop on the far side of the booksellers.

"How are you today, Lillibet?" Moira asked with a smile, her own troubles momentarily forgotten.

"All right, miss—my lady," Lillibet replied, blushing furiously as she twisted the corner of her relatively clean apron. She started to sidle back into the shadow of the shop, as if she was afraid to be seen talking to Moira.

Considering who her father was, that might indeed be so.

"Are you still going to have the school, my lady?"

"Yes, Lillibet, I am. They've started to work on it already." She nodded to a stand of trees on the northern side of the village. "Just over there, in that grove. You can go look at it if you like. I'm counting on you to be one of the first students."

"Oh, no, my lady, Pa says school's a waste o' time for the likes of us," Lillibet demurred. "We should be out earnin'. Maybe Jackie will be able to go someday. He's a clever wee bairn, my lady."

Jackie was only three years old. Knowing how fiercely Lillibet's father opposed the school, it might take that long to persuade him to change his mind. "I hope that once it's built and other children begin to go, he'll decide to send *all* his children."

Lillibet nodded, yet Moira could see disbelief that such a thing would ever come to pass in the little girl's hazel eyes. "I'd better get along home now," Lillibet said softly as she dipped a curtsy, then rushed away.

If only there was some way she could make Lillibet's father see that education was not a waste! Moira thought as she watched her go. Learning provided a window onto the wider world, and surely there was nothing wrong with that.

More determined than ever to build her school and somehow convince Big Jack MacKracken and all those other parents that the school would be good for their children, Moira started toward the livery stable again.

And realized there was nobody outside it, or the tavern, where there was usually at least three or four men gathered, unless it was raining.

She stopped and looked around and discovered that men were gathering in the nearby meadow. They looked excited, not anxious. Then she saw the empty square of space about eight feet on all sides, marked off with ropes and stakes.

That could mean only one thing: there was going to be a prizefight.

She was relieved her father had declined to come to Dunbrachie with her that day. Attending a boxing match inevitably led to celebratory drinking if the man her father had wagered on won, or consolation drinking if he lost.

She hoped Jem and the two footmen weren't in the

crowd, although she supposed she could fetch them if she had to. First, though, she would see if they were inside the livery stable.

As she continued on her way, the tavern door opened and two men came out—Sir Robert McStuart and another man dressed only in a kilt. He must be one of the boxers. He certainly looked strong enough, with broad shoulders and muscular arms, and the kilt offered a view of legs that were just as powerful. He was barefoot and she recalled her father saying once that fighting barefoot made it easier to maintain one's balance. He also wore no hat, and his tawny hair waved—

Her jaw fell open. Sweet merciful goodness! It was Gordon McHeath!

She ducked into the nearest doorway and stared. Even the embraces they had shared had only hinted at the magnificent, virile body beneath his clothes. Now there was no need for guesswork.

Desire and need surged through her anew. He looked like one of those Greek or Roman statues, only made of flesh and blood and vibrantly alive.

After the two men had passed on the other side of the street, and as if her feet had a will of their own, she turned and followed them toward the field.

Chapter Nine

Moira hadn't gone twenty feet before she stopped. It would be completely inappropriate for a lady to watch a prizefighting match. Given that there was already so much gossip about her, she ought to avoid doing anything else that would cause more scandalized whispers, thinly disguised innuendos and curious stares, no matter how much she wanted to see if Gordon McHeath was indeed going to engage in a prizefight. After seeing him rush down that hill, recovering from his spill with athletic grace and especially after seeing him half-naked, she was rather sure he'd be able to hold his own in the ring, or anywhere.

Still, it would be exciting to witness the contest....

No, she must not.

With a reluctance equal to her disappointment, she started back toward the livery stable—until she saw the Three Geese slipping into the milliner's shop.

Her first thought was that they must have seen Gordon McHeath. Her second was that Sarah Taggart was a good friend of the milliner, whose family lived on the second floor. Sarah and her friends must be planning to watch the match from the upper windows.

Her third was that it was too bad she couldn't join them.

Sighing, she continued on her way, past the milliner's and the lane between it and the bookseller. It was like the lane where she'd been with Mr. McHeath, except that this one had several empty crates taking up much of the space toward the rear, where there was also a lean-to attached to the milliner's shop.

Moira paused and looked more closely. If she piled some of those crates on top of each other, she could climb onto the top of the lean-to and from there to the roof, where she could see the meadow, and the match.

It wouldn't be a ladylike thing to do, but if she were careful, no one would be able to see her on the roof.

A swift survey of the market revealed that no one was looking her way. Their attention was either on the meadow, or trying to get a bargain, and some of the merchants and peddlers had already started packing up their goods. Sam Corlett had put away most of the trimmings that had decorated his wagon and was moving with haste to finish the rest, glancing frequently at the crowd gathering in the meadow.

Moira ducked into the alley. Once more glad she'd spent all those hours clambering around her father's warehouses like a monkey, she began piling the empty crates that had likely held books or pamphlets. Whatever they'd held, she was relieved she was wearing her gloves so she wouldn't get splinters. When she had a sufficient pile, she hiked up her skirt and petticoat and put one booted foot on the bottom crate. Holding her breath, she grabbed hold of a crate two levels above and pulled herself up.

The pile shifted a little, but not enough to fall. Now she could reach the edge of the roof of the lean-to, and holding tight to it, she climbed another level of crates. Again they shifted, but again they held. Finally she managed to get onto the top of the lean-to.

Panting, she had to wait a bit to catch her breath, then got on her hands and knees.

Her skirts were not going to make the rest of her plan easy to put into effect, but she hadn't spent all that time climbing without learning a thing or two about dealing with feminine clothing. After first making sure nobody was in the lane, she started to roll her skirts until they were about midthigh, and fastened one side into a knot to hold them. Her dress would be wrinkled, but hopefully only the servants would see that when she returned.

Once her skirts were secured, she carefully made her way up onto the roof of the milliners. She had to go slowly, for it would be disastrous if she fell or dislodged a piece of slate.

She obviously wasn't as strong as she used to be; nevertheless, she wasn't going to let her own weakness defeat her. At last she reached the ridgepole and peered over the peak of the roof. She could indeed see into the meadow, as if she were a bird flying overhead.

"Isn't he marvellous?"

Sarah Taggart's voice was as clear as if she were beside Moira on the roof.

They must have opened the window below to see better.

"He'll win. I'm sure of it, even against the Titan," Emmeline Swanson declared.

Moira nearly let go. Everybody in Dunbrachie and the surrounding villages had heard of that particular boxer, who weighed three hundred pounds at least and had left a trail of broken bones and bruises in his undefeated wake.

This was the man Gordon McHeath was going to box?

Had he taken complete leave of his senses?

Regardless of the wager he'd made, despite the possibility that winning this fight would make Robbie drop his suit, he never should have agreed to this, Gordon thought as he followed the excited and more-than-half-inebriated Robbie toward the makeshift ring. He should have come up with a better way to end the lawsuit, or simply refused to represent Robbie anymore and gone home to Edinburgh.

Coming to Dunbrachie was proving to be as great a mistake as believing Catriona McNare cared for him, and being alone with Lady Moira at any time was obviously an even worse one.

He also should have kept on his shirt and trousers rather than accepting the tavern keeper's offer of this old kilt. That would have been warmer and more modest, and would it have really mattered if a pair of trousers and shirt got ruined in the mud that was sure to be churned up?

"I'm to be your bottle man," Robbie reminded him as they drew near the excited crowd composed entirely of men. "The tavern keeper's son's going to be your knee man. He's fetching the bucket with a sponge."

Gordon nodded absently. The knee man would go down on one knee so the fighter could use his thigh as a stool between rounds, rounds that would only end when one of the two fighters got knocked to the ground.

He hoped it would be a short fight, and thank God Lady Moira wasn't here to see this barbaric spectacle. At least, he hoped she wasn't here, but he wasn't about to scan the crowd, either, because if she was…

If she was, the die was cast and there was nothing he could do about it.

"Well, where's your champion?" Robbie asked the man with the bright yellow vest, who was waiting in the ring.

In daylight, the fellow looked even more seedy, with a day's growth of dark whiskers on his face, squinting eyes and a greasy hat pulled down over his forehead.

Beside him was a slender fellow in his late teens wearing a brown wool greatcoat and hat and holding a bucket with a ladle. There was another bucket at his feet, with a large sponge in it for wiping a fighter's face. On his other side was a short, beefy fellow whose wide thigh could probably hold both Lady Moira and Lady Catriona McNare at once.

"Let's just get started, shall we?" Gordon said, anxious to get this over with.

"Keen to have your nose broken, are you?" the seedy fellow said with a cold laugh. "That's the Titan's specialty, so I'm sure he'll be happy to oblige."

Robbie hadn't told Gordon anything about his opponent—nor had he asked, which might, Gordon realized with a sickening feeling in the pit of his stomach, turn out to be another colossal blunder. Nevertheless, Gordon kept his voice impartial as he replied. "Titan? As in, father of the gods? Am I to assume my foe is a supernatural being?"

"Never mind what they call him," Robbie said quickly—too quickly. "You can beat him with your eyes shut."

"You can try," the man with the yellow vest said with a smirk, "but they don't call him the Titan of Inverness because he's a wee lad." He nodded across the ring. "Here he comes."

Gordon *really* wished he hadn't agreed to fight when he saw the man they called the Titan of Inverness. His opponent might not have passed for an Olympian god, but if somebody had told Gordon this was a son of Hercules, he might have believed it. The man was easily six foot six and had to weigh over three hundred pounds. Not only that, not an ounce of his weight appeared to be fat. He could probably pull an oxcart full of rocks all by himself. His eyes were little slits in his broad face; his head was bald as an egg and shaped like one, too. Like Gordon, he wore only a kilt; no shirt, boots or stockings.

He was, without doubt, the largest, most unsettling opponent Gordon had ever seen, let alone faced in the ring.

The Titan strode to the center of the square and regarded Gordon with a raised brow, as if to say, "This is the best you can bring against me?"

Gordon was equally silent as he marched out to meet his enormous adversary. Instead of facing the man, though, he walked around him, studying the Titan, seeking any weakness or vulnerability and making the Titan crane his neck to see what he was doing.

A hush fell over the crowd. The Titan held out his hand. Gordon shook it and then let go, signaling the start of the match.

The Titan immediately lashed out with his longer arms. Fists up defensively, Gordon leaped back. Fortunately he was light on his feet—certainly lighter than a man the size of the Titan would be. Yet he mustn't assume that would be a winning advantage, not when the man had that long a reach, plus strength and experience, as well as no qualms at all about breaking his opponent's nose and probably any other bones, as well.

The Titan's right arm shot out again. Gordon ducked and moved in for a quick jab at the area of the man's kidneys. He hit the Titan hard, but the fellow barely seemed to feel it.

Gordon danced backward. The Titan followed, moving with more speed than Gordon expected. He nearly got hit in the face, only avoiding the blow by instinct. He dodged another rapid strike, then lashed at the Titan's jaw.

He didn't connect, yet the way the man reared back gave Gordon sudden hope. Some men could endure blows anywhere but the jaw, and a strong punch there would knock them flat.

The only trouble was landing a good, strong punch to the more easily defended face.

If he could tire the Titan, Gordon reasoned, he would be less able to defend himself. That meant he had to keep the man moving.

And Gordon had to stay on his feet.

That wasn't easy, not when the Titan kept him bobbing and weaving to avoid his massive fists.

The Titan moved him back to the edge of the ring. He lunged and struck Gordon's right shoulder. Gordon fell backward, landing hard on his rear.

"End of round!" Robbie shouted.

He and a lad of about sixteen rushed toward him, helping him to his feet and toward their corner. He was especially glad to have the chance to sit and catch his breath, and take a long drink of cold water from the ladle Robbie held for him.

"You've got him, Gordo," Robbie whispered in his ear. "Man's as slow as a turtle."

Had Robbie actually been watching?

"He can't keep up with you for much longer!"

Gordon wasn't sure he could keep up with the Titan much longer, either.

"Watch his fists," Robbie added.

Gordon didn't bother to respond to that unnecessary advice. He scanned the crowd, seeing no familiar faces and certainly no female ones.

He glanced up at the sky, trying to judge the time. About two in the afternoon, he made it, so it would get warmer yet.

As he lowered his gaze, he saw something that made him think he was hallucinating, despite not having been hit in the head. Either that, or someone wearing Lady Moira's bonnet was lying on the roof of a shop on the other side of the green.

He blinked and wiped his face, but before he could look again, Robbie shoved him to his feet.

And a new round began.

"Oh, surely it can't last much longer, can it?" Mabel Hornby cried.

Still lying on the roof, Moira wondered the same thing as she watched the two men circle each other yet again. The bout had already lasted at least an hour, to judge by the changing shadows. Both Gordon McHeath and his opponent were bleeding and bruised and had been knocked down more than once, although Mr. McHeath had been on the ground less than the man she knew only as the Titan of Inverness.

The Titan was huge, seemingly all brawn. Fortunately, Mr. McHeath was faster on his feet and often deftly eluded the blows. He also managed to make his fewer strikes more effective.

By now, though, both men were showing signs of wearying and she feared McHeath would soon be too tired to avoid a crushing punch from the Titan's beefy fist.

Nor should she stay here much longer, lest her father

start to wonder where she was. But she didn't want to leave until she knew who had won the fight.

She hoped it would be Mr. McHeath—because he seemed so outmatched yet was holding his own, or so she tried to convince herself.

"Papa told me of a boxing match that went for fifty rounds," Sarah Taggart said, her voice quivering with excitement, as if she wanted to see this fight go at least as long.

"Oh, dear!" Mabel Hornby replied. "I do hope—"

Whatever she hoped was lost in the roar that went up from the crowd as Mr. McHeath, kilt swirling, dodged another blow aimed at his face.

None shouted so loudly or enthusiastically as Robbie McStuart. Judging by his flushed face and the way he kept taking swigs from the jug in his hand, he wasn't just excited, he was drunk. Moira wouldn't be surprised to discover he had wagered on the outcome, too.

How could she have missed the signs of his weaknesses for so long? How could she have been so blind she hadn't realized the kind of man he was from the first time she met him at the ball they'd hosted shortly after they'd arrived in Dunbrachie?

Even though being a lady was new and wondrous, and he was charming and flattering, she should have paid more attention, and been much more careful.

At least she'd never been intimate with him. She'd never even kissed him, except for a few mild kisses on the cheek. She'd told herself that Robbie was treating her the way a lady ought to be treated and she should be glad. Only later had she realized he probably didn't feel much desire for her.

And today, she'd been made to see how little she'd desired Robbie, compared to the passion Mr. McHeath aroused.

Yet if she hadn't become engaged to Robbie and broken that engagement, she might never have met Gordon McHeath. Never been helped by him, or kissed by him, or met him in a secluded lane and discovered that although he should be her enemy, all she wanted to do was—

The Titan suddenly jabbed, catching Mr. McHeath in the gut. Moira gasped in dismay as the solicitor fell hard on his knees. But in the next moment, McHeath's fist flew up, connecting with the Titan's jaw. The big man stumbled back. McHeath leaped to his feet and struck again with a series of jabs to the face and chest that soon had the Titan sprawled flat on his back, his eyes closed. His legs moved and she feared he was going to get up, but it was like watching a man trying to swim on dry land before he gave up the effort and stayed still.

He had won! Mr. McHeath had won!

He staggered away from his fallen foe, while Robbie McStuart shouted with glee as if he'd won the fight himself and didn't care how battered and bruised his friend might be.

As the Three Geese chattered and giggled and talked about Mr. McHeath's victory, Moira began to climb gingerly down from the roof. She would have to come up with some excuse to explain the state of her clothes, even to the maid, but that didn't worry her. It had been worth wrinkling her gown to see McHeath win.

Wearing nothing but a kilt.

"You came out of it better than I would have imagined," the gray-haired local doctor said as he finished dabbing at the cut over Gordon's eye with witch hazel.

Although the short and stocky Dr. Campbell looked more like a butcher or baker than a man of medicine, his movements were deft and his touch light and gentle. His hands were also clean, Gordon was pleased to note, his beard well trimmed and he exuded an air of calm competence that Gordon appreciated as he sat on a bed in an upper room of the tavern.

Sounds of merriment and Robbie's laughter, as well as the smell of roast beef and bacon, wafted up through the floorboards from the taproom below. The mud-splattered kilt lay on the floor nearby, and Gordon was once again attired in his own clothes.

"I never would have guessed a solicitor would want to be a prizefighter, too. I should think you have enough conflict in your life, doing battle in court or wrangling over contracts," the doctor noted with a wry smile.

"I do," Gordon agreed, wincing at the sharp little pains that even Doctor Campbell's light ministrations couldn't prevent. "Participating in the match wasn't my idea."

"Ah," the doctor said, his smile shrinking to a frown. "Sir Robert's?"

"Aye."

The doctor drew back and regarded Gordon gravely.

"A word of advice there, my young man. I've seen Sir Robert's sort, and they are very good at not only going astray themselves, but taking others with them. I would be very careful if I were you."

"I shall be," Gordon assured him. He grimaced as the doctor dabbed at the cut over his eye. "Especially after this."

"Good, because you're lucky you weren't more badly hurt," the doctor said as he stopped dabbing. "None of your bones were broken and you have only a few cuts and bruises. I've tended to others the Titan's fought who came out of it much worse."

"How is the Titan? Not badly hurt, I hope," Gordon said, having asked the doctor to check his opponent first.

"Not bad at all," the doctor replied as he finished putting the witch hazel and leftover bandages back into his black valise. "He's below in the taproom, holding court with Sir Robert. I daresay he's not saying much of anything about today's fight, though. More likely he's reliving past glories."

Gordon rose with slow deliberation, reached into his jacket and pulled out his wallet. "How much do I owe you?"

The doctor named a very reasonable sum, which Gordon gladly paid.

"You'll be a little sore for the next few days," the doctor advised, "but otherwise, you should be right as rain soon. Now I give you good day, Mr. McHeath, and I wish you a safe journey back to Edinburgh."

"Thank you, Doctor," Gordon replied as the man departed.

The solicitor pulled on his jacket and made his way to the stairs. Judging from the raised voices, the Titan wasn't the only person holding court below. Robbie had obviously had more to drink—something that became even more obvious when Gordon entered the taproom and saw his friend lounging in a chair by the hearth, with a barmaid on his lap.

Chapter Ten

"Gordo!" Robbie cried, pushing the barmaid off his lap and sitting up straighter.

Instead of looking annoyed by his cavalier treatment, the freckled, brown-haired barmaid giggled and sashayed toward a keg to fetch more ale for another table of men clamouring for her attention.

"All tended to, I see," Robbie said, running a satisfied gaze over Gordon. "Come and have a victory drink—on me, of course."

"Robbie, it's time to go," Gordon said, wondering how much of his winnings Robbie still had, if any.

"It's the shank of the evening!" Robbie protested, setting his wineglass down with a bang. "I was just going to tell them about the time you stole that money and—"

"I'd prefer you didn't," Gordon snapped. His shame and the mistake that could have altered the course of his life for the worse weren't just a funny anecdote to him. "I'm tired and sore, and you've had more than enough to drink already."

As Robbie's brows lowered ominously, Gordon realized he shouldn't have let his frustration get the better of him and spoken in haste.

"You can go if you wish, but I'm staying," his friend said with an all-too-familiar glint of stubbornness in his eyes.

Once Robbie got that look, no power on heaven or earth would change his mind. Robbie would stay and drink until he passed out, even if it took all night.

"Very well, then," Gordon said, declining to argue or try to persuade him. "I'll see you in the morning."

Or not, because I'm leaving for Edinburgh at dawn and you had better honor your promise or....

Or what? He had no power over Robbie, or what he might do. All he could control was his own involvement with Sir Robert McStuart, and he would decline to have any more.

So Gordon decided as he walked out of the tavern, ignoring the protests of some of the other patrons and Robbie's claims that his friend had always been a grim sort of fellow. He headed straight for the livery stable, where Robbie's driver waited near the barouche, along with other drivers and grooms and linkboys.

"Sir Robert intends to stay awhile yet," he told the driver. "You might as well wait in the tavern."

"What about you, sir?" the driver asked. "Are you staying, too?"

"No. I'll walk." He was tired, but used to walking,

and McStuart House wasn't more than a mile away. Besides, Robbie was going to need the carriage more than he did.

"It's looking to be a cold, damp evening and the night air's not good for a body," the driver warned, and others around him nodded their agreement, showing more concern for Gordon's health than Robbie had. "Are you sure you don't want me to drive you? I can come right back for Sir Robert afterward."

"No, thank you. I do appreciate your concern," he sincerely replied. "I know the way, and it's not far. I'll risk the night air."

In no small part because it would be fresh and clear, not redolent of ale, smoke and beef. "I'll take a torch, though," he added.

One of the linkboys offered his. Accepting it with thanks, Gordon started walking down the road toward McStuart House.

It was indeed a damp, chill night for a walk, but the sky was clear and the moon so bright he really didn't need the torch. Indeed, it was proving rather heavy, his arms being fatigued from the match, so he put it out in a puddle in the ditch along the side of the road and carried it by the middle of the shaft in his left hand, swinging it as he walked.

With his bandaged right hand he put up the collar of his jacket and winced at the effort. His clients in Edinburgh would surely wonder what had happened to his face and hands; he doubted any of them would come right out and ask, though.

He would certainly never tell them.

He flexed his right hand before he shoved it in his pocket. Thank God he'd still be able to write, and that he'd gotten the better of the Titan. One solid blow from that man to his head and he might have been seriously hurt.

How would Lady Moira feel if she heard he'd been injured? Would she be sorry? Or would she think it was no more than he deserved for agreeing to fight?

And for representing Robbie. For being Robbie's friend. And for his impetuous, brash embrace and passionate actions in the lane.

He came to a halt and drew in a deep, cold breath. Ever since Robbie had proposed the fight…no, ever since Robbie had told him he wanted to sue Lady Moira for breach of promise, he'd believed he was better than Robbie. Now he had to face the truth. He wasn't, as his recent lascivious behavior with Lady Moira proved. He was just as lustful, just as weak, just as selfish. Just as shameful.

A dark shape bounded onto the road in front of him, then stood, legs braced, blocking his way.

For one heart-stopping moment, he thought it was a wolf.

It wasn't. The head was too big. It was a dog baring its teeth and growling. That same big black dog that had chased Lady Moira up a tree.

Gordon moved the unlit torch to his right hand, ready to use it as a club, if necessary.

A sharp whistle cut the air. The dog lifted its head, growled once more, then loped away into the underbrush.

Once it was gone, Gordon let his breath out slowly. Where had it come from? Who owned the beast, for clearly it had responded to a summons from someone? Whoever it was, that animal shouldn't be allowed to roam freely.

He should ask Robbie's butler who the constable of Dunbrachie was, and he should write to him to tell him about that menace of a dog, he thought as he started on his way again. This time, though, he looked around as he walked, and kept the torch in his right hand, just in case.

He had gone about fifty yards when he caught the flicker of a light out of the corner of his eye and turned to scrutinize the trees on his left. Yes, there was a light, deep in the wood beyond the road, and in the same direction that the dog had gone.

Maybe he could find out who owned the dog and what they were doing in the wood. Not that he would risk approaching anyone in such circumstances directly, but he could get a little closer, enough to hear voices and names, perhaps. There might be more than one person with the dog, and until he knew their purpose here, he had best be careful and not be seen.

As he left the road and started toward the light, he discovered a narrow road leading in that direction, the ruts muddy from recent use. Perhaps it was a Gypsy encampment, although they likely would have been at the market, trading or offering to tell fortunes, and he hadn't seen any there.

Moving slowly and quietly, he reached the edge of a clearing and saw two men, one holding a torch, standing near a stone building with a pile of wooden planks beside it. The man with the torch was remarkably short. His dark brown coat was dirty and patched, his trousers so old they hung on him like a bag. His companion was taller, dressed in a jacket and better-fitting trousers, boots and a scruffy cravat. More noticeable than his clothes was his hair, which was thick and red, and so was his beard. The dog stood near the shorter man.

"What are you waiting for?" the taller man said, making no effort to speak quietly. "Burn it. Burn it all."

He wanted his companion to set fire to the wood? That would surely damage the building, too, if not set it alight. Or was that their intention?

Good God, was he witnessing attempted arson?

Fearing that he was, Gordon turned, ready to run back to Dunbrachie for help—until something struck him hard from behind. With a gasp of pain, he dropped the torch and staggered forward. Meanwhile, the dog charged at him, as fierce and frightening as a wolf. Another blow landed on his shoulder. The other two men came running, the bobbing torch making strange shadows leap and dance.

Gordon half turned and put up his arm in self-defence as another blow from a thick branch came toward his side. He was too slow, and before he could avoid another, his assailant—older, grizzled, dressed in rough homespun—swung his weapon again, this time catching Gordon's thigh. His breath came out in a whoosh as he went down on one knee. The dog grabbed his sleeve, worrying it as if it were a rat or badger.

He tried to stand up, but the dog held him fast. He crouched and covered his head with his arm as the branch came down on his shoulder again. He opened his mouth to call for help; all that came out was a croak. With a mighty effort, Gordon twisted, turned and wrenched his sleeve free of the dog's sharp teeth. He had to get away. He had to get back to the road. The tavern. Find help.

The branch came down again as he stumbled to his feet. This time, though, he was ready and grabbed the weapon, pulling it away from the grizzled man with a mighty yank. The bearded man got hold of him. He squirmed to free himself—and then he felt something hot and stinging in his side, like the bite of a big insect.

The bearded man let go and Gordon fell to his knees, his hand to his bleeding side. God help him, he'd been stabbed.

The heavy branch came down again, striking Gordon hard across the shoulders and he fell forward, landing facedown in the mud.

These men were going to kill him...unless they thought he was already dead. That might be his only chance.

Barely breathing, Gordon lay still, regardless of the dog taking hold of his sleeve again, or the blood seeping from his side, or his aching head and body.

He had to remain conscious. He didn't dare open his eyes, yet he had to get all the information he could so they could be brought to justice. When he survived. If he survived.

"God damn it, Red!" one of the men growled in a Yorkshire accent as somebody pulled the dog off him. "You've bloody killed him. We'll get the noose now for sure if we're caught."

"We aren't bein' paid to do murder," another voice muttered, his accent more Midlands than Yorkshire. "Give some noblewoman a scare, burn the school, get paid and go, that's all."

This was Lady Moira's school? And three men had been *paid* to burn it? And frighten Lady Moira, too? Who would do such a…?

God, surely not Robbie! It couldn't be. Robbie wouldn't be that vindictive. He couldn't have changed that much…could he?

"Go if you're scared, but you give up your share if you do," the Scot, who must be Red, grumbled.

"Who was he?" the man from the Midlands asked.

A foot shoved Gordon until he rolled over, limp as a rag doll. "I'll be damned, it's McStuart's friend, the fella who beat the Titan."

"Maybe they'll think that's what done him in," the Yorkshire man suggested.

"What? The Titan came after him and stabbed him? Not bloody likely," the man from the Midlands muttered. "What was he doing anyway?"

"Maybe he was drunk. Maybe they'll think he was robbed by some passing highwayman or summat," the Yorkshire man said.

"If we hide his body somewhere, we can be paid and

gone before he's even found," the Scot suggested. "Then we'll be in the clear for sure and certain."

Without any further discussion, someone took hold of Gordon's wrists and dragged him over the rough ground, every inch a torture. The smell of damp earth filled his nostrils, and his shirt was soaking with wet mud and blood.

The man let go of his arms and gave him another shove with his boot, sending Gordon rolling down a short slope until he was lying in a ditch or little gully. He continued to lie still, although he was half in a puddle and so cold and damp, he started to shiver.

Mercifully, the men who attacked him didn't notice, perhaps because it was too dark, and they moved away. The wind rose, rustling the remaining leaves of the trees around him, sending droplets of water onto his already-wet clothes and hair.

Cold, wet, in pain, bleeding, drifting in and out of consciousness, he tried to stay awake, to listen for sounds of the men leaving.

Then the wind brought the smell of smoke and the snap and crackle of burning wood.

They'd set fire to the school.

He tried to get up on his hands and knees. If he could crawl, maybe he could get to the road, and if he could get to the road, he could fetch help. He could save the school. He had to save her school....

Although it was past midnight and Moira was dressed in her fine linen nightgown and sky-blue silk bedrobe, her thick hair in a long braid down her back, she hadn't been able to sleep. Her mind was abuzz in a way that made sleeping, or even lying down, impossible.

It was more than worry about her father and what he might be doing. He'd gone on another business trip to Peebles and wouldn't be back until tomorrow afternoon, or so he'd told the butler, and so Walters had informed her when she returned from the market in Dunbrachie. Her father had said nothing to her about business in Peebles but just because he hadn't told her about his plans earlier, that didn't mean he was meeting some of his old cronies to play cards and drink. Or so she hoped.

It wasn't frustration that Big Jack MacKracken and his cronies didn't want her to build her school, or dismay over anything Sarah Taggart had said. It wasn't the lawsuit Robbie had brought against her.

What kept her awake tonight was confusion about Mr. McHeath's feelings and behavior when they were together, and her own.

What was it about him that stripped her of all restraint? she wondered as she paced restlessly in the large room that faced south and overlooked the gardens and wood.

It couldn't be just his looks and form, although they were impressive. After all, she'd met other good-looking men before, business associates of her father, or their sons, or other social acquaintances, for she had many friends in Glasgow. And Robbie McStuart was considered extremely good-looking. Yet she'd never felt for any other man even a tenth of the desire that Mr. McHeath aroused.

No doubt their first meeting, when Mr. McHeath had behaved so chivalrously, accounted for some of the difference, she supposed as she stirred the coals in the fireplace, making the flames rise a little higher and the room a little brighter.

At night, this room was about as comfortable and cozy as a cave, even with a fire in the tiled hearth. Despite the presence of oil lamps and candles, every corner was dark with shadows. The mournful cries of peacocks in the garden added to the gloomy atmosphere, and not even the furnishings from their home in Glasgow could give her much comfort.

The armoire had been her mother's, and her writing desk had been a present from her father when she was ten years old. One of the chairs by the tiled hearth had been her grandmother's, and her father had bought the landscape of a mountain meadow covered in heather that was hanging over the mantel on a business trip to the Isle of Skye.

During the day, and especially when the sun was shining, the room was much more pleasant. Then she could see the brighter colors of the wall covering decorated with oriental birds and flowers, and the large windows revealed a pleasant landscape, instead of looking like tall pools of ink.

But it was night, not day, as she put the poker back into its stand and drew her bedrobe more tightly about her. She sat in her grandmother's chair now upholstered in cream-colored silk, the same chair where she'd spent several other anxious nights waiting for her father to stagger in the door, drunk and jovial.

He was always jovial when he was drunk, and always in an ill temper the next day. He wasn't mean or cruel, only quick to anger or take offence, something that had cost him more than one business transaction or customer. If he hadn't been so good at striking bargains, his business would have suffered; mercifully, so far, it had not. But if he broke his promise to her again, how long might it be before it, too, was affected?

With a heavy sigh, she rose and went to the window to draw back the green velvet draperies with gold fringe. If only her father was home. If only he didn't have a weakness for drink. If only she had never met Sir Robert McStuart, or accepted his proposal. If only Gordon McHeath had never come to Dunbrachie. Then she might have peace and contentment…except that she would never have experienced the incredible thrill and excitement of being in Gordon McHeath's arms. She would never have felt that heated desire, those amazing sensations or shared those passionate encounters….

Her grip tightened on the fringe of the drape. She mustn't think about such things. She must remember that Gordon McHeath was Robbie McStuart's friend, and even if he seemed sympathetic to her, he was nevertheless helping Robbie McStuart to sue her.

Off to the east, the sky glowed over the site of her school. At least the building would soon be completed, and she could console herself with that. Of course, the patronizing Mr. Stamford might not make it as easy a process as it should be, but hopefully he'd learned—

That wasn't where the sun should rise.

Years ago there'd been a warehouse fire down by the docks in Glasgow. The sky had glowed just like that.

Her school!

She ran to the door and threw it open. "Fire!" she shouted at the top of her lungs. "My school's on fire!"

Chapter Eleven

They were too late.

By the time Moira and her men—grooms, footmen, stable boys and gamekeepers—got to the site of her school on horseback and in one of the wagons, all that was left of the stone building and pile of wood waiting to be used were smoke-blackened walls, charred beams and smoldering remains.

As Moira regarded the ruins, she tried to take some comfort from the fact that many of the men from the village had come to try to help put out the fire. It was clear they had rushed from their beds, dressing in haste and grabbing buckets and shovels.

Since it was obvious there was nothing more to be done, the villagers began to leave. A few offered their condolences, but most began to drift away without speaking directly to her, leaving her to mourn in silence.

"'Tis a terrible thing, but it could have been worse, my lady," the head groom said. "Thank God the trees and undergrowth were damp with the mist from the river, and the building wasn't closer to the trees, or more than your school might have gone up in flames tonight."

"Aye, it could have been much worse," she agreed. "I'm glad no one was hurt."

"Must have been tramps or Gypsies, I reckon, taking shelter and their fire got out of hand," Jem offered. He pointed to the end of the pile of ashes that had once been lumber intended for the interior. "It started here, looks like, out of the wind. Good spot for shelter, behind the wood."

"I haven't seen or heard of any Gypsies hereabouts," Moira replied, rubbing her arms for warmth in the damp air. "There were none at the market."

"Tramps, then," Jem said with a decisive nod.

Moira wished she could be so confident that some wandering vagrant had accidentally set the building alight. Unfortunately, she'd heard too many objections to the school to believe it couldn't have been someone who lived in Dunbrachie, like Big Jack MacKracken.

Would he have gone that far? Would he have been willing to run not just the risk of imprisonment and transportation, possibly even hanging, by burning down more than the school? If the trees had caught fire, homes and shops might have been destroyed, as well. Many in Dunbrachie agreed with him that her school was a mistake, and others were his neighbors. Would his anger have gone so far that he would put them at risk of losing property and perhaps even their lives to stop the school?

Or could the bitter Robbie be vindictive enough to do something like this? Had she been even more mistaken about his character?

"My lady! Over here!" one of the grooms shouted from the edge of the clearing. "There's somebody here in the ditch!"

Gathering her skirt in her hand, Moira ran to the spot and scrambled down the small embankment to the muddy bottom. The groom was bent over a man lying on the ground beneath a thick bramble bush, his clothing soaked and muddy, and his hair—

She recognized that hair.

"It's Mr. McHeath!" she cried, kneeling beside him and gently rolling him onto his back. She could scarcely breathe herself, for fear that he was dead.

He moaned.

Alive, thank God! Alive!

Yet he was far from well. There was an ugly, bloody gash over his right eye and fresh bruises colored his chin and cheek. Worst of all, there was a huge bloodstain on his shirt, bright and fresh.

"Jem, see if you can find some boards or branches to make a stretcher," she ordered as she slowly shifted until Gordon McHeath's head rested on her lap. "And send one of the boys for the doctor. Have him come to the manor. Quickly now!"

"Aye, my lady."

"Send someone for the constable, too," she added

as she brushed the wet, muddy hair from Gordon McHeath's pale brow.

"You're going to be all right," she whispered fervently as she looked down at his cut and bruised face. "You're going to be all right!"

"God damn it, that was close!" Rafe gasped as he lay panting on the moldy mound of hay in the loft of an abandoned outbuilding on the Earl of Dunbrachie's estate. "I ain't run so fast since I nearly got nicked pickin' pockets in York."

"We wouldnae cut it so close if that lawyer hadn't come," Red Mac MacCormick said as he hunkered down in the corner, his back to the wall.

"Here's hopin' they don't find him for a while yet," Charlie said as he tossed a hunk of bread down to his dog below. The animal snapped it up in one bite and sat on its haunches waiting for more.

"How long do ye reckon we'll have to stay here?" Rafe asked, scratching at a fleabite.

"Till the man comes with the money," Red replied.

"Tomorrow?"

"Maybe," Red said, taking out his dirk and wiping off the blood with a handful of hay. "He'll have to wait until nobody's watchin' him."

"Better be soon, unless you've got some food stored hereabouts," Rafe replied before he started to cough.

"If he don't come today, we'll go to him," Red declared. He nodded at the oldest among them. "Charlie here knows all about housebreakin'. He can get us in."

Charlie frowned as he tossed another hunk of bread to his dog. "Not likely," he said, his voice low and rough.

"You can't, or you won't?" Rafe demanded.

"Too risky," Charlie replied. "Too many servants."

"Then that's it," Red said. "We wait here."

"And get caught, like as not—and then he don't have to pay us at all, or ain't you two thought o' that?" Rafe asked harshly.

"He's good for it, I tell ya," Red retorted. "But if you want to live like a beggar the rest o' your miserable life, go. And good riddance."

Rafe got to his feet. "Not without the money I was promised. Not when I might swing for helpin' you."

The dirk still in his hand, Red rose and faced him.

Sweat beaded Rafe's grimy forehead as he began to back toward the edge of the loft. "I only want what I'm owed. What I was promised. Easy money, you said. Well, where is it then?"

Charlie muttered something under his breath.

"What'd you say?" Rafe demanded, his frightened gaze flicking from the man with the knife to the man whose dog would rip out a man's throat on command.

"I said, if we let you go, maybe you'll turn us in for a reward," Charlie said.

Rafe shook his head and took another step back. "I won't. I just want to get out of here with my life, and never see neither of you again."

"I dinnae think we can let you do that, can we, Charlie?" Red said with a sidelong glance at his companion.

"Nay," Charlie said. He got to his feet and pulled off his leather belt.

The dog waiting below began to growl low in its throat. Red took a step forward. Charlie began to wrap his belt around his right hand.

Rafe took another step back. To the very edge of the loft. Crying out, he flailed his arms and tried to get his balance. Failed.

And fell.

The next morning, sunlight streamed into the east-facing windows of the Earl of Dunbrachie's manor house. Outside, birds sang and sheep grazed on the expansive lawn as if nothing at all had happened last night. Inside, the servants attended to their tasks almost as if this day were like any other, although not quite. There was too much excitement and avid speculation whenever two or more met and spoke in hushed whispers about the fire and the man who'd been brought back in the wagon using Lady Moira's lap for a pillow and what looked like her petticoat wrapped around his torso.

When Moira and Mr. McHeath had arrived at the earl's residence after what had been the most harrowing journey of her life, Moira had ordered her servants to carry Mr. McHeath to the blue bedroom, the most spacious one aside from her father's. Using warm water and clean linen, she'd done the best she could to wash the mud and blood from his face. She'd used her petticoat to try to staunch the bleeding before they'd moved him from the ditch and had been afraid to remove it or do anything more until the doctor arrived.

That had been at least an hour ago, and she had been walking the floor of her morning room ever since.

Once this had been her favorite room in the manor of the Earl of Dunbrachie. She had chosen a delicate paper depicting green, fernlike plants, and the furniture was light oak with mahogany inlays. The chairs and sofa were upholstered in a light green silk and pictures of the Scottish countryside hung on the walls.

Here she had believed a new and wonderful life was about to begin, of comfort and ease, parties and balls.

Here she'd dared to hope her father would never again indulge in too much drink and she would know peace and happiness.

Here Robbie had proposed.

Here she had broken their engagement.

And now here she waited with her heart in her throat for news about whether Gordon McHeath would live, or die.

Who had attacked him and why? Given how he'd rushed to her aid the first day they met, perhaps he'd come upon whoever was setting the fire and tried to stop it, or at least call out an alarm.

Whatever had happened, it had been near her school, and she felt responsible. She must and would see that everything possible was done for him.

She remembered the first time she'd seen him, when he came rushing down the ridge to her rescue. How handsome he was, how brave, how like a hero from a fairy tale.

She recalled the first time she'd touched him, when

she'd jumped from the tree. The strength of his arms. The security he seemed to offer.

She vividly remembered the first time they'd kissed— that heated rush of desire, and the shock of mutual passion. It was a kiss like no other, until the second.

She would never forget the wondrous excitement awakened by his caresses and the vitality of his body, a vitality that surely must survive whatever injuries had been inflicted upon him.

A man cleared his throat.

She whirled around to find the butler standing on the threshold. "Is Mr. McHeath…?"

She couldn't say the word. Didn't even want to think it.

"Dr. Campbell says you can see him now, my lady," Walters said.

She nearly fell to her knees with relief, but since Walters was there she only drew in a deep, shuddering breath and said, "Thank you," before hurrying from the room as fast as dignity would allow.

Once at the top of the stairs, she took a moment to catch her breath before entering the blue bedroom, then put her hand on the latch and went inside.

Although the heavy velvet draperies had been opened to allow the sunlight to enter, she couldn't immediately see Mr. McHeath or the doctor. A screen painted with a scene of a medieval hunt had been put around the bed made of oak during the reign of Charles II and curtained with pale blue silk trimmed with gold.

The rest of the furniture shone in the bright morning light—the armoire inlaid with mahogany and hazel and polished with beeswax, the pedestal table near the hearth, the washstand by the door to the dressing room. The glass in the lamps sparkled, and the thick Aubusson carpet muffled her steps as she ventured around the screen.

Dr. Campbell sat beside the bed. The instruments and accoutrements of his profession, bottles of ointment and salve and his black valise, were on a small side table nearby. A basin full of bloody water and another containing several soiled linen cloths sat on the floor nearby.

She looked at the man lying so still in the bed.

Mr. McHeath was very pale, except for the bruises on his cheek and chin. The cut above his eye had been bandaged. His hair, damp with perspiration, clung to his forehead. He'd been carefully dressed in a nightshirt, and his chest rose and fell with his breathing.

He was alive, at least, and she must and would cling to that.

"Doctor?" she said softly, afraid to disturb either one of them.

Dr. Campbell glanced over his shoulder, put the bottle he was holding into his bag, rose and faced her.

"How is he, Doctor?"

"As well as can be expected, all things considered," Dr. Campbell answered, his voice sympathetic, his eyes grave. "Fortunately, I can detect no broken bones. However, he's been stabbed and—"

"Stabbed?" she gasped.

"Yes, and he's lost a considerable amount of blood.

Luckily, the knife grazed the rib and missed any major organs or arteries."

Or he would be dead.

The doctor took her arm and led her to a chair near a slightly open window. "Please, sit, my lady."

"I'm…I'm all right," she muttered, although she really felt sick and dizzy. "I'm just so…"

Relieved and terrified. Upset and hopeful. Worried and appalled and frightened and glad.

As the doctor looked down at her, he took her hand gently in his. "There is more, my lady. I fear he may have suffered a concussion. It may be serious, it may not. The longer he remains unconscious, though, the greater the possibility that serious damage has been done. It's also difficult to ascertain the extent of any internal injuries to the rest of his body. Infection and pneumonia remain a danger, especially since we don't know how long he was exposed to the elements. He has a low fever that may indicate that infection has already set in and if it has, the outcome could be fatal."

Fatal.

She wouldn't despair. She couldn't. He had to get better. He simply had to.

"I must also tell you that I don't think he should be moved for a week at the very least. And he should have a nurse. There's a woman in the village, Mrs. McAlvey, who's very skilled."

Finally something she could do—or at least pay for. "You must do whatever is necessary, Doctor, without any concern for the cost."

"Excellent. I'll send Mrs. McAlvey here as soon as I

return to Dunbrachie." He gave Moira a consoling smile. "You must try not to worry, my lady. He's a strong young man, so I think we can have good cause to hope that he will make a full recovery."

Moira nodded.

Leaving her by the window, Dr. Campbell returned to packing his bag with swift, efficient motions. "I was sorry to hear about your school, my lady. What a terrible thing!"

"My school can be rebuilt," she said, looking at poor Mr. McHeath lying so still.

"You intend to do so?"

She hadn't really thought about it, but after he asked the question, she made her decision. She wasn't going to let rogues and vandals destroy her dream. "I do."

The doctor picked up his valise. "I regret I cannot stay any longer, but Mr. Monroe is very ill and I must see how he fares today. I'll send Mrs. McAlvey as soon as possible. In the meantime, if Mr. McHeath doesn't wake up soon, try to rouse him. If you cannot, or if he wakes but falls asleep again and you cannot wake him after a few more hours have passed, send for me. Or if his fever worsens."

"Yes, Doctor."

He started for the door, then turned back. "Is your father here? Perhaps I should apprise him of Mr. McHeath's condition, as well."

"He's away on business," she replied, for once glad that he wasn't at home. Even if he were, he wouldn't want to speak to Dr. Campbell, about anything. Ever since her mother had died less than a day after a doctor had pronounced her illness nothing more than a slight congestion in the chest, he'd lost all respect for the medical profession, or anyone who practiced it.

"Good day, then, my lady."

Once the doctor had gone, Moira sat by the bed and picked up a square of fresh linen that smelled of lavender, one of the many little luxuries their new life afforded. She dipped it in the ewer of cool fresh water and wrung it out.

She was about to wipe Mr. McHeath's forehead when he suddenly shifted and mumbled, "Why didn't you tell me?"

Although he was talking, his eyes were still closed and when she called his name, he didn't respond.

He moved again. "You should have told me."

"You must rest, Mr. McHeath," she said softly as she wiped his forehead. "You've been very badly hurt."

His eyes abruptly opened and he reached out to grasp her arm with surprising strength. But his gaze was unfocused and his next words told her he wasn't really aware of where he was or to whom he was speaking. "I loved you…I thought I loved you…but now I don't know… and Robbie…what's happened to Robbie?"

"He's not here," she said, desperately wondering if she should leave him to call for help, or stay where she was.

Before she could move, Mr. McHeath started to sit up. "I don't love you. I never loved you. I thought I did, but I didn't."

She put her hands on his shoulders to push him back

down. "Lie still, Mr. McHeath!" she ordered. "Lie still!"

His eyes closed and panting heavily, he obeyed. Then his eyes flew open again, and although they were still glassy and unfocused, he stared at her as if he was seeing a ghost. "Catriona?"

He moved as if he meant to try to sit up again. She could only think of one way to get him to lie still.

"Yes, Gordon, I'm here," she said, moving to sit beside him on the bed and taking his overly warm hand in hers. "You must lie still and try to sleep, so you'll get well again."

"Catriona," he sighed, his eyes drifting closed. "Why didn't you tell me there was someone else?"

"Hush, now, Gordon," Moira said. "You must rest."

"You should have told me!"

"Shh, now, Gordon, please!" Moira insisted as she held his hand and caressed his perspiring cheek.

"You should have told me," he repeated as he turned his head away from her. "I thought you cared for me, but all the time... All the time there was..." His voice began to trail off in a rough rasp. "Somebody else. Not me. Not me..."

With her free hand, Moira reached for a fresh cloth to wipe his brow. Catriona, whoever she was, must be a fool—ten times ten a fool if she would reject Gordon McHeath's love and devotion for some other man. Why, *she* would give anything...

"I need to go away," he murmured. "Robbie. I'll visit Robbie. He's a good friend."

If Robbie McStuart was a good friend, she'd hate to meet a bad one.

"She's beautiful. And brave. Climbing up in a tree."

Her breath caught. Had the unknown Catriona ever climbed a tree?

"I wanted to kiss her…such kisses… Moira…."

He was talking about her!

"I want…"

Chapter Twelve

What? What did he want?

Holding her breath, Moira waited for him to answer, but it seemed Mr. McHeath wasn't going to speak again, or wake up, either, at least not immediately.

Who was this Catriona he'd talked about? What did he mean when he spoke of only thinking he was in love?

Would she ever know? Perhaps not, but finding out the answers was less important than his recovery. If only she could somehow heal him with the power of her mind and…and…deep affection.

Remembering how her mother used to check for fever, she half rose, leaned over and gently kissed his brow.

He was cooler! Wasn't he? She was about to try again when he stirred and his eyelids fluttered open. He turned his head very slightly toward her and looked at her, and this time, she thought he really saw her.

Then he whispered, "Moira?"

Never in all her life had she been so glad to hear her own name!

"Yes!" she cried with relief and excitement. Surely this was a good sign! Surely he would get well! "Yes, it's Moira! Oh, Gor—oh, Mr. McHeath! How do you feel? Are you in pain anywhere?"

He licked his dry lips. "Thirsty."

She immediately poured him a glass of cool water and sat beside him, raising his head and holding the glass to his lips as she cradled his head in her arm.

He managed to drink some of the water before he began to splutter. She quickly set the glass down, then eased his head back onto the pillow.

She tried to be gentle, but he winced nonetheless. "What…what happened?"

He didn't remember? Was that a bad sign? "You were attacked. You were found near the school and we brought you here, to my father's house."

He closed his eyes, and for a moment she feared he'd lost consciousness again, until his brow furrowed and he quietly said, "I remember now. There were two men, one with a torch. And that dog that chased you. They were going to burn the school. I…I was going to get help." He opened his eyes and his anguished expression nearly undid her. "I didn't succeed, did I?"

Whether he'd managed to summon help or not, her heart filled with gratitude for the attempt as she answered in a whisper. "No. By the time anyone realized the building was on fire, it was too late to put it out. I'm sorry my school was burned down, but I'm more sorry you were hurt."

His gaze held hers for a long moment as she tried to think of a way to express her thanks for his effort, but in the end could only say, "Thank you for trying."

He looked at the foot of the bed and began to move his legs as if attempting to get up. "I should go."

She immediately put her hands on his shoulders and held him down. "No, you mustn't. Not yet. Doctor's orders."

"Doctor?" he repeated with a frown.

"Of course we sent for the doctor," she said, still holding his shoulders, unwilling to let go, or let him go. "You've been badly hurt. You mustn't think of leaving here for a few days, until you're feeling better. Given what you tried to do, our hospitality is the least we can offer."

At last he stopped struggling. "You're…too kind."

He spoke as if she were being completely selfless. She wished that were so, but if she were being completely honest, she would have to admit she was happy to have him here, where she could watch over him and make sure he recovered. Where she could see him and spend time with him.

Before he went back to his life in Edinburgh, far away from Dunbrachie. And her.

"Well, now, where's my young man?" a middle-aged, plump, pleasant-faced woman carrying a worn valise demanded as she marched into the room like a captain assuming command of a ship.

An obviously distressed Walters followed in her wake. "I beg your pardon, my lady. I tried to make her wait until I could announce her, but she insisted upon coming up the stairs immediately."

"Bless you, no need for announcements," the woman replied as she went to the side of the bed. "I'm the nurse, of course, Mrs. McAlvey." She set down her valise and cocked her head to one side as she studied Mr. McHeath, who was just as intently studying her.

"That will be all, Walters," Moira said as she watched the two of them, one young and handsome and sick and wary, the other older, broader, matter-of-fact and… smiling?

"Well, he looks better than I expected, all things considered," Mrs. McAlvey declared as she took off her cloak and handed it to Moira without any regard for class or rank. She also spoke as if Mr. McHeath was still unconscious, even though he was looking right at her. "I've seen plenty hurt worse than him be right as rain after a week or two."

"I'm delighted to hear it," Mr. McHeath said, a tad louder than he had to and obviously a little disgruntled at being spoken of as if he wasn't aware of her presence. "I'm feeling better already."

However dismayed Mr. McHeath might be, Moira wanted to hug her. Mrs. McAlvey had surely been around enough sick and injured people that her opinion could be trusted.

Not a whit disturbed by Mr. McHeath's disgruntled

remarks, Mrs. McAlvey gave a hearty laugh. "A pity you look like a dog's breakfast, then," she said to him. She put her hands on her hips. "So, you're the fella beat the Titan of Inverness. Well, you've got the shoulders for it, although I can't say I ever heard of a lawyer making a bit on the side prizefighting."

"I wasn't paid a penny."

"No? Good heavens, man, you should have been, by all accounts. Most entertaining boxing match in years, they're saying in Dunbrachie. Still and all, I trust this'll be the last time. We aren't none of us getting any younger." She glanced at Moira. "Now, as delightful as I'm sure this young man is finding your company, my lady, it's time for you to go. The man needs his rest—and you should have a nap yourself. Dr. Campbell said that seeing you got some sleep was part of my job, too."

Moira didn't want to leave, but she doubted there was anything more she could do to help Mr. McHeath now that the capable and voluble Mrs. McAlvey was here.

She was nearly at the door when an even more distressed Walters arrived.

She immediately thought of one reason for his demeanor and hurried out of the blue bedroom, closing the door behind her. "Has my father come home?"

And is he drunk?

"No, my lady," the butler replied, giving her some temporary relief from her dread before he gave her another cause for concern. "Sir Robert McStuart is below and wishes to speak with you."

Never had she been more tempted to have the butler tell someone she wasn't at home. However, Mr. McHeath was Robbie's guest, and Robbie deserved to know that his friend was here, as well as his condition. He also had to be told that Mr. McHeath must stay where he was until the doctor said otherwise.

As she went down the stairs, it occurred to her that Robbie might have been worried about Mr. McHeath's whereabouts last night. He might have spent several anxious hours wondering where his friend was or what had happened to him—although if that had been the case, he should have had men searching for him, and clearly he had not.

Her suspicion that Robbie hadn't been overly concerned about his friend's absence proved unfortunately correct, for instead of finding Robbie anxious and upset, the young aristocrat stood by the drawing room windows with legs planted, arms akimbo and his expression angry.

One look at his face and she could guess where he'd spent the night. His eyes were bloodshot, his complexion pasty and he was swaying enough to suggest that if he hadn't been drinking already this morning, he'd had enough last night to keep him semidrunk today. His clothes looked as if he'd slept in them, as perhaps he had, and he smelled like a brewery.

"What's happened to Gordon?" Robbie demanded as soon as he saw her. "One of the lads from the village said he saw him in a wagon heading this way with his head in your lap."

As if she and Mr. McHeath had been involved in some sort of illicit activity, and as if that was worse than Robbie's apparent neglect of his friend's safety, letting him go back to McStuart House alone. "He was attacked and left for dead near what is left of my school."

Robbie stared at her as if he couldn't quite comprehend.

"You do know about the fire? Mr. McHeath came upon men setting fire to my school and tried to stop them. He was beaten and stabbed."

His mouth gaping, Robbie felt for the end of the sofa and sat heavily. "Of course I heard about the fire. Everybody was talking about it," he whispered hoarsely, as if it hurt his throat to speak. "And then the boy told me about Gordon. I thought he'd gone to help put it out and gotten too much smoke. But you say he's been beaten? And stabbed. He's not…he's not…dying?"

Seeing his genuine distress, her heart softened a little toward him. "No, thank God."

Robbie covered his face with his hands. "I never should have let him leave alone!"

No, he shouldn't, but that couldn't be changed now. "Fortunately, he's awake and coherent and getting the best of care, so I think he'll be all right in a few days."

Robbie raised his distraught face to look at her with pleading eyes. "You mean that?"

As if she would lie to him about such a thing. "Aye. The doctor said there's good reason to hope he'll recover."

"Thank God, thank God!" Robbie muttered as he leaned forward and clasped his hands in a prayerful attitude.

"I assume he has family in Edinburgh who should

be informed of what's happened and that his return will be delayed."

"What? Oh, no, Gordon's parents are dead and as far as I know, he doesn't have any other close relatives. There's Mitford, who's handling his business in his absence—Gordon told me that when we were playing chess. I'll write to him."

"Thank you, Robbie."

Robbie sighed and shook his head. "I shouldn't have stayed in the tavern last night. I should have gone home with him or insisted he take my carriage."

Yes, he should have, but that was not what was most important, and she had to ask, even if she doubted she'd get an honest answer. "You didn't know about the fire before it was set, did you?"

Robbie straightened as abruptly as if she'd punched him. His eyes narrowed and his face flushed. "You think I had something to do with that? You honestly think me capable of such a thing?" He leaped to his feet before she could answer. "Good God, if you believe that, no wonder you broke our engagement!"

His arms crossed, he continued to glare at her. "I assure you, my lady, that whatever you think of me, I had *nothing* to do with that fire, or the attack on my best and dearest friend. And it's not as if there aren't plenty of other people to suspect. There are several I could name who might have decided that setting fire to the school was the best way to stop the arrogant Lady Bountiful from taking over the education of their children."

He came a few steps closer. "What, you don't think

you're arrogant? What else is it when you presume to tell other people what's good for them?"

That wasn't what she was doing at all! Besides… "Education is always beneficial!"

"Not when it's forced down people's throats," Robbie retorted.

"I haven't forced anybody to do anything!"

"No," he scornfully replied, "you've just made them feel like ignorant peasants."

Good heavens, was that possible? Could she have done that? That had never been her intention.

"Yet you presumed to call me arrogant and selfish when you broke our engagement," he went on. "What are you but the same, although you cloak it in the mantle of good works?" He came closer, forcing her to step back. "You think you're so much better than me—aye and everybody else. You think you have all the answers, know how everybody ought to live. Well, you *don't!* You don't know anything, you presumptuous, naive witch! Now take me to Gordon. He's coming home with me."

His harsh, unfair, cruel words only served to invigorate her, not intimidate her. "No. The doctor says he can't be moved."

"Is that so—or do you think keeping him here will stop the lawsuit? I assure you, it won't. I'll sue you with or without Gordon McHeath."

She had never truly hated Robert McStuart until this moment. It wasn't what he called her, or the anger and hatred in his voice and face. It was his accusation that she would use such base tactics to win the lawsuit, an accusation made seemingly without a particle of genuine concern for his friend's welfare. "Get out of this house, Robbie," she said, her voice low, but firm in its purpose. "Get out and *never* come back."

"You can't—"

"I have several footmen I can summon," she said, heading for the mantel, and the bellpull.

Robbie muttered a curse, turned on his heel and left.

He heard voices.

Hushed, whispering voices. That nurse's was the loudest. And there was a man. Gordon didn't recognize his voice at all.

Wasn't that Lady Moira speaking?

It was *her* voice—that soft, dulcet, beautiful voice— that had summoned him back from a deep well of pain before. He'd opened his eyes and discovered her looking down on him with…great affection.

He opened his eyes. Yes, she was there, at the foot of the bed, standing beside a middle-aged man dressed in black with a very grim expression. He was also balding and had very bushy gray eyebrows. Behind them, looking like a warden standing guard over two prisoners and with her arms folded over her ample bosom, was Mrs. McAlvey.

"He's awake," she announced.

Yes, he was—his aching side and head proved that, for he'd felt no pain in his dreams.

He'd been dreaming about Catriona at first, and his folly. Then Moira had been with him, bold and brave and kissing him.

"We didn't mean to disturb you, Mr. McHeath," Lady Moira said, "but if you're able, Mr. McCrutcheon, the constable, has some questions for you."

Of course. He should have been expecting a representative of the law to arrive.

"I'll try," Gordon said. He started to sit up, until the pain in his side put an end to that. "I suppose you want descriptions of the men who attacked me."

"For a start," the constable confirmed.

"There were three." Gordon described them as best as he could remember, including their accents. "And there was a dog. A big black dog."

Lady Moira started, and he nodded. "Yes, the same dog. Lady Moira and I had an earlier encounter with the beast," he explained to the constable. "I saw the dog last night, then some light through the trees. I wanted to find out who owned the dog, so I went after it toward the light, as carefully and quietly as I could in case it was a band of vagabonds or other unsavoury sorts. I heard one of the men order the other to start the fire. Before I could summon help, I was struck from behind. The other men joined the attack, the red-haired one stabbed me and I thought they'd kill me unless I played dead, so that's what I did. They dragged me to the ditch and left me. I tried to get up but I couldn't."

"You were too badly hurt," Lady Moira said softly.

"And a good thing you didn't, too, or you'd be dead for sure," Mrs. McAlvey declared. "If they hadn't done for you, the bleeding would have."

"I overheard them talking," Gordon went on, wanting to tell the constable everything he could remember while the memories were relatively fresh. "They'd been paid to set fire to the school."

"Paid?" Lady Moira repeated incredulously. "By whom?"

How he wished he had an answer to that, so that they could find whoever was responsible and stop him, and keep her safe! "I'm sorry. I don't know."

"Paid, eh? Well, that's a different sort of bagpipe," the constable mused aloud. "That makes it likely they weren't from around here at all. No wonder nobody recognized him."

"You've captured one of them?" Lady Moira asked eagerly.

Gordon had asked enough questions himself in his legal practice to recognize when somebody had revealed more than they meant to, and the constable had just done so.

Nevertheless, he answered Lady Moira. "Aye, we've got one o' 'em. The Yorkshireman, by the sounds of it."

Gordon also had enough experience to recognize when a person was only revealing a part of the truth. "Who is he?"

"We still don't know."

"I think that's just about enough questions for now," Mrs. McAlvey said. "The man needs his rest."

"Just a few more," the constable replied, his tone as decisive as hers. "Mr. McHeath, during this struggle, did you have a weapon of any kind?"

"No."

"Did you take one of theirs, or pick up a stick?"

"No."

"What would it matter if he had?" Lady Moira demanded. "Surely he had a right to defend himself."

"Aye, so he did—and so he did."

Gordon's head was throbbing now, and it was difficult to make sense of what the man was saying. "What do you mean?"

"The man we found—he's dead."

Chapter Thirteen

"Dead?" Moira gasped, while Mr. McHeath blinked like a man who'd been submersed in water. "How?"

"Hit on the head from behind, looks like," the constable replied.

"That'd do it," Mrs. McAlvey grimly agreed.

"And you think...you think *I* killed him?" Mr. McHeath asked.

Then his eyes rolled back.

"That's enough, Mr. McCrutcheon!" Moira cried as Mrs. McAlvey rushed to the bedside and immediately felt Mr. McHeath's forehead.

Mr. McHeath's eyes opened again and he started to speak—but whatever he had to say could wait.

"You've answered enough questions today, Mr. McHeath," Moira said firmly before she turned to the constable. "Come along, sir."

"I appreciate you're upset, my lady," Mr. McCrutcheon

said as he followed her from the room, "but these questions have to be asked."

"Not now, not if they cause a serious setback for Mr. McHeath," she replied.

"How do you know it was Mr. McHeath who hurt the man?" she asked as they went down the stairs. "Perhaps the vandal injured himself running away."

The constable shook his head when they reached the foyer. "I doubt it. The doctor will have to take a look to say for certain, but it looks like he was hit from behind with something heavy—a shovel handle or piece of wood, perhaps."

"Even if Mr. McHeath killed that man, surely no court would consider him guilty of murder or even manslaughter," Moira said, facing the man who was also the village undertaker. His arrival had given her another shock, until she'd remembered that. "Whatever happened, he was attacked by men committing a crime and he had no weapon with him, so it was clearly self-defence."

The constable looked as if he'd rather be anywhere else. "I'm not saying it wasn't, my lady, and I'd expect a man like Mr. McHeath to put up a fight, but there'll still have to be an inquest when he's well enough to give evidence."

At least the constable was willing to be reasonable, and so, therefore, was she. "I'm sure he'll be glad to testify eventually," she said in a more serene manner. "What about those other men he described? Have you found any trace of them?"

"Not yet, but if they're still around Dunbrachie, we will," Mr. McCrutcheon answered staunchly.

They wouldn't if they'd already fled, and if they'd done what they'd been paid to do, she doubted they would stay in the vicinity. Or they might, if they'd been paid to make more mischief.

It was all getting to be too much. Mr. McHeath attacked, her school burned down, Robbie suing her, her father… "If you'll excuse me, Mr. McCrutcheon, I'd like to rest."

"Aye, my lady, it's been a long night and day for you, I'm sure. There's just one question I need to ask you. Can you think of anyone who would pay to have your school burned down?"

She had already dismissed Big Jack MacKracken because that fire could have endangered the rest of Dunbrachie. Now she was sure he couldn't be responsible, because he certainly wouldn't have the money to pay anybody to do anything. And while Robbie McStuart could afford it, he had seemed so genuinely upset….

That Gordon was hurt. Not that her school had been destroyed. "Sir Robert has been very angry with me for breaking our engagement."

"Oh, I doubt it was him, my lady," the constable replied evenly.

She should have realized that a man whose family had wielded power and influence in a village for generations might be considered above suspicion, for anything. There was no point protesting unless and until she had proof he was the person behind it. "If not Sir Robert, I can't think of anyone else."

"Well, good day to you, then, my lady. You be careful now, won't you?"

"I will," she assured him.

Feeling as if she hadn't slept in a week, Moira went back upstairs. She knocked softly on the door of the blue bedroom, which was soon opened by a sympathetic Mrs. McAlvey. "He's sleeping like a baby, my lady. I can wake him up easy enough, so don't you worry. He's going to be fine, or my name isn't Martha. You go on and have a nap yourself. You wouldn't want him to see you with circles under your eyes, would you?"

Moira warmed with a blush, but she didn't disagree. She didn't want Mr. McHeath to see her looking tired or upset.

If she were wise, she thought as she went to her own bedroom, she wouldn't let him see her at all. She would keep her distance from him, if only for her own peace of mind.

And heart.

"Well now, that's better, I'm sure," Mrs. McAlvey said as she briskly tucked the blanket around Gordon the following morning. "All clean and tidy and looking much more like a gentleman than a prizefighter," she added with a wink.

He was glad to hear it. It was bad enough he'd been in that fight; he didn't want his face to appear as if that was the way he earned his living.

"I'm sure Lady Moira will be happy to see you so well."

"I'm very grateful for her hospitality—and her father's, too, of course."

"Oh, yes, it's the earl you're so anxious to see," Mrs. McAlvey said with a chortle that grew into a laugh. "Don't be lookin' at me like that, young man. I've been nursing for twenty years and if you can't learn about people in that time, you're a dolt. Now you just have a nice nap, and you'll be all refreshed when her ladyship comes round to see you."

"She may not," he replied. "I'm sure she has better things to do."

Mrs. McAlvey reached into the valise at her feet and pulled out some knitting that looked like either a small blanket or a large muffler, in a rather eye-popping shade of scarlet. "She may, but she'll come round nonetheless. She's the sort worries about everybody, especially them that she feels responsible for, and she feels responsible for you."

"She shouldn't, and I'm truly sorry for any trouble I've caused her."

"Oh, I don't think she's upset about having to look after you. It's her father. He's gone off again, probably more than half in his cups somewhere, like as not." She regarded Gordon with a raised brow. "Surely a fellow in your profession can see there's something amiss with the man."

"I've never had the pleasure of meeting him."

"Well, if you had, my buck, you'd know from the first glance that he drinks too much and it's gone to his liver. His nose is red and his eyes have that yellow tint gives it away. I realized the man was a tosspot the first time I saw him in the village—and so has Dr. Campbell. But there's not much he can do if the man won't come and see him."

If the earl drank to excess, like Robbie, it was no wonder Moira had rejected his friend.

And he sympathized with her. He'd had more than one client who overimbibed, and he saw the havoc it created for families—the uncertainty, the bitterness, the resentment, the chaos, the quarrels, the rage.

Despite the sudden pain that made him gasp, he threw off the covers and started to get out of bed.

"Here now! What do you think you're doing?" Mrs. McAlvey demanded.

"Getting up," he replied, although he felt dizzy and sick when he moved, and his side burned as if it were on fire.

But he couldn't stay here, not if it meant trouble for Moira, and conflict with her father. After all, he'd prepared the initial papers for the lawsuit. Of course the earl would want him gone at once.

The miracle was that Moira hadn't.

"Oh no, you're not," Mrs. McAlvey exclaimed, pushing him back down. "You've had a bad blow to the head and you'll open that cut in your side, you great daft git!"

He tried to sit up again, but she held him down, and she had the strength of the Titan, or so it seemed. "I have to go!" he insisted.

"Not yet! You know what the doctor said—or do you want to have a relapse, maybe even kill yourself? That'd be a fine way to thank the young lady!" Mrs. McAlvey declared as she examined the bandage at his side. "You *have* opened that wound! I'll have to rebandage it. It's going to hurt, but it's no more than you deserve for disobeying the doctor, and me."

Open wound or not, he had to leave.

"Stay still!" Mrs. McAlvey barked as she started to undo the bandage. "Whist, the blood's dried and this is going to stick."

And then she tugged. He yelped from the pain—and everything went dark.

Later that day, after Mrs. McAlvey told Moira that Mr. McHeath shouldn't be disturbed but she could see him tomorrow, Moira rode along the road leading to her school. Since those two men and that dog hadn't yet been found, she wasn't alone; Jem and another groom rode behind her.

She wanted to survey the damage before she met with Mr. Stamford to decide what ought to be done next.

As they traveled through the wood, the sun peeked out from behind high clouds and the song of birds broke the quiet. It was so lovely here, away from the dust and grime of the city. And peaceful, too, when all was well.

In spite of recent events, she felt happy, and not just because Mr. McHeath was recovering. A brief note from her father had arrived while she was napping. Although all it said was that he had arrived safely in Peebles and would be back before the end of the week, she could take comfort from the fact that if he was with his cronies who led him astray, he wouldn't have written at all.

She was also sure it would be better if he stayed away until Mr. McHeath was well enough to go to Sir Robert's. Her father wouldn't be pleased to have Mr. McHeath for a guest.

He would likely be even more upset to discover his daughter secretly wished she could change places with Mr. McHeath's nurse. *She* wanted to be the one to lay a napkin over his chest before he ate, to change his bandages, to cover him, to talk or simply sit in silence as he healed.

A pony cart came into view.

A pony cart driven by Sarah Taggart, and she had her two friends with her. As usual, Miss Hornby had on a bonnet with far too much ornamentation, and too little in the way of flattering colors for her complexion. Miss Swanson had on a prettier ensemble of Nile green, and Miss Taggart's pelisse was of superfine wool in a lovely shade of blue. If only her personality could be as nice as her taste in clothes!

Had Moira been alone, she would have ridden off the road into the trees to avoid them. Since she wasn't, she had no choice but to remain where she was and be exquisitely polite.

"Good day, Miss Taggart, Miss Hornby, Miss Swanson," she dutifully greeted when the cart came abreast of her horse.

"Good day," Miss Taggart answered, apparently for all three. "Oh, dear, you have had a time, haven't you? You look utterly done in."

If ever wolfish derision was clothed in the sheep's wool of sympathy!

"How is poor Mr. McHeath? I do hope he wasn't too badly hurt!" Miss Hornby said, interrupting the chilly silence.

Moira had always thought Mabel Hornby would make a good friend if she weren't a satellite of Sarah Taggart. "He was quite seriously injured, but he's getting better, I'm happy to say."

"So he'll be leaving you soon?" Sarah Taggart archly inquired.

She made it sound as if Moira and Mr. McHeath would be ending an affair, and Moira didn't doubt she meant it as a jab. Her arrow went far wide of the mark, though, for instead of making Moira angry, it elicited exciting images of being in bed with Gordon McHeath. Being naked with an equally naked Gordon McHeath. Being intimate with him. Touching and kissing and caressing.

"I said, will he be leaving you soon?" Sarah repeated more forcefully.

"As soon as he's able," she replied, her fantasy acting as a most effective calming agent, so that Sarah's attempts to upset her seemed like the pesky buzzing of a harmless insect. "He has to wait for Dr. Campbell's permission."

"How fortunate for you. He must be most *fascinating* company."

"He's a very interesting man," Moira agreed, "but of course I want him to get well as quickly as possible." She gave Sarah her most empty smile. "Don't you?"

"Naturally," Sarah snapped as a blush reddened her cheeks.

"You're lucky you'll get to keep him for a while longer," Emmeline said, as if he were a pet, "since he'll have to be well enough to travel to Edinburgh before he can leave."

"He need only be well enough to go to McStuart House," Moira corrected.

"Oh, dear, she doesn't know," Sarah said with a smug glance at her friends.

"She must not," Emmeline agreed.

"We only learned about it ourselves," Mabel noted, earning her a censorious glance from Sarah.

"Sir Robert's not in Dunbrachie," Sarah announced with a superior air, as if Moira must be stupid not to know his whereabouts. "He's gone to Edinburgh. On business, I understand. *Legal* business."

Moira waited for Sarah to make a snide remark about the lawsuit.

It didn't come.

Instead, she said, "There's a rumor going about that he wants to sell McStuart House. He must not want to stay where there are so many *unpleasant* memories."

Relieved that Sarah was still ignorant about the action for breach of promise or she surely would have mentioned it by now, Moira had a few darts of her own to launch. "Perhaps he's so ashamed of his behavior, he thinks he should sell his family's home and never show his face here again. Obviously there's nothing and no one here to tempt him to stay."

Sarah's lips curved up in a most unladylike and ugly scowl before she delivered a vicious slap of her reins on her pony's rump. The poor beast gave a startled whinny and took off down the road. With a little shriek, Emmeline Swanson grabbed her bonnet and Mabel Hornby clung to the side of the cart for dear life, although she also managed to call out, "Give Mr. McHeath our best wishes!"

As the cart disappeared around a bend, Moira realized the men behind her were stifling guffaws. She smiled, too, for a moment. Then she sighed as she thought of Mr. McHeath going back to Edinburgh.

Where he belonged. And she did not.

There was nothing she could do about that. There was something she could do for the children of Dunbrachie, however, so she nudged her horse to a walk and continued toward the charred remains of the school, although that was not uppermost in her thoughts. Why was Robbie leaving Dunbrachie? How could he even think of selling his ancestral home…unless he had to. But why? The scandal of their broken engagement affected her far more than him.

Why else would a man sell his family home?

Because he no longer wanted it?

In Robbie's case, that was unlikely. He'd been too proud of that house, and its history. He'd been so happy showing her all the portraits and explaining who was who in the family tree.

Why else?

A house such as that took a lot of money to maintain. And Robbie spent a lot of money, on entertaining and clothing. Was it possible he no longer had the funds to maintain it?

And if he was lacking the money for that, how

desperate might he be for funds? Desperate enough that he would want to marry a wealthy man's daughter?

If so, wouldn't that make the breaking of that engagement even more devastating for him? That would explain so much….

They were about fifty yards away from the ruins of the school when she saw something that made her rein in quickly and signal for her men to be quiet.

Somebody was already there.

Chapter Fourteen

"Who are you and what are you doing here?" Moira shouted, her grip tightening on her reins.

His face and hands and clothes black with soot, Big Jack MacKracken came out from behind a half-fallen wall.

"Why are you here?" Moira demanded as her men rode up beside her and Jem reached for his riding crop.

Big Jack didn't answer. He stood where he was and, to Moira's even greater surprise, Lillibet came around the wall, her face and hands and clothing equally dirty. She smiled up at her father before saying, "We're cleaning away the burned wood from inside, my lady."

Moira wouldn't have believed that explanation if Big Jack had been here by himself. Since Lillibet was with him, it seemed more plausible. Unfortunately, however, as she knew from sad experience, a daughter might be all too willing to make excuses for an errant parent's behavior.

"Is that so, MacKracken?" she asked, nudging her horse a little closer.

"Aye, my lady," he said, his face reddening beneath the soot as he twisted his equally filthy cap in his big hands.

She halted her horse and, after a moment's hesitation, dismounted. "I thought you didn't approve of my school."

"Well, my lady, it's like this," the big man began, shuffling his feet like an embarrassed lad. "I didn't hold with it, but that don't mean I'm willin' to let some ruffians come to Dunbrachie and burn anything. Seems the least I can do is offer a bit of a hand with the cleaning up."

It was a start, anyway. "I'm grateful for your help," she answered sincerely. She was about to offer to pay him, when Robbie's stinging words about being an arrogant Lady Bountiful came to her mind. "Thank you."

Nevertheless she simply couldn't let this opportunity to speak on behalf of his children pass without further comment. "Perhaps when my school's rebuilt, you'll let Lillibet come. She's a very clever girl—just the sort any shopkeeper would be happy to hire if she could read and do figures."

"I'll think on it," Big Jack muttered, glancing down at his daughter, who looked up at him as if she'd just been given a seat at a banquet.

Moira didn't press him further. "Will you show me what you've done?"

"Aye, my lady," he replied with a nod.

* * *

"A most excellent recovery," the doctor said two days later as he packed up his medical bag after examining the bandage over Gordon's eye and his side, leaving his patient to gingerly button his nightshirt. "I think another day or two, and you should be able to ride in a carriage. Not if it goes a gallop, of course, but a nice leisurely journey should be possible."

"Thank you, Doctor, for your excellent care," Gordon replied, knowing he should sound happy, even if he wasn't.

Well, he was glad to hear he was healing; he wasn't so happy to hear he could leave, even though he had no right to stay.

Mrs. McAlvey, standing near the door, delicately cleared her throat. "I had a most excellent nurse, too," Gordon said.

"Indeed, you have. Mrs. McAlvey is one of the best."

The older woman justifiably beamed. "I'll be glad to continue, if you need my help when you go home."

"Thank you," Gordon said.

"Ah, my lady!" the doctor exclaimed as Lady Moira herself appeared on the threshold.

As always, she was simply but exquisitely dressed, her glossy brown hair modestly styled, her gown a day dress of pale green sprigged muslin. Most beautiful of all was her shy smile, yet it was even more thrilling to know that beneath that bashful exterior lurked an amazingly passionate woman.

Even though she had only looked in on him briefly

at night and in the morning for the past two days, his admiration and desire had not diminished. If anything, his appreciation for her excellent qualities and his own passionate yearnings had increased, so that he longed for those few brief moments in her company or even just a glimpse of her smile.

"I don't know what you've been feeding this young man," the doctor declared, "but his recovery is remarkable. Mr. McHeath should be quite fit to travel in another day or two."

"So soon?"

He mustn't attach any significance to her surprised query. Or think that was disappointment in her doe-brown eyes. He'd learned the folly of thinking a woman's reaction or expressions meant more than they did. Hadn't he?

"If he wishes," Dr. Campbell confirmed.

And he really had to go home. "My clients were expecting me to return in a fortnight," he said as much to himself as to her and the others.

"Sir Robert came when you were first brought here and he said he would inform someone named Mitford," she replied.

How difficult it must have been for her to talk to Robbie—another debt he could likely never repay. "Mitford's a solicitor friend who's working with my clients while I'm away. But he has his own practice, so I shouldn't be away longer than necessary."

Even if he wanted to.

He couldn't gauge her reaction to that.

"Will Mr. McHeath be well enough to travel all the way to Edinburgh, Doctor?"

The doctor's brow furrowed. "I had assumed he would be returning to Sir Robert's."

Before Gordon could correct him, Lady Moira said, "Sir Robert isn't at home. He's gone to Edinburgh."

Gordon stared at her in surprise. Why had Robbie gone there? Had he decided to tell Mitford what had happened in person—or did he have another, more self-centered reason for going? A debt? A woman? Because he simply wanted to?

Gordon could believe any or all of those explanations might be the right one.

"Is that so?" Dr. Campbell said as he closed his black leather bag with a snap. "In that case, I would recommend that Mr. McHeath stay here another few days."

"Not if my presence is an imposition," Gordon said quickly, resolved not to be a burden for Lady Moira, or cause her any more trouble.

"You're most welcome to stay," she said, her voice calm and even, without enthusiasm—or reluctance, though, either.

Dr. Campbell's glance went from one to the other before he said, "I'll see myself out," and started for the door.

"I'd like a word with you, Doctor, about what Mr. McHeath ought to be eating," Mrs. McAlvey said, following him.

"Of course."

After the doctor had gone out, the older woman paused and looked back from the doorway, her expression grave, but her eyes shining with sympathy, making her as beautiful as an angel of mercy as she addressed Lady Moira. "However Mr. McHeath may be acting, he's still weak as a kitten so you should only stay for a little while, my lady. Nobody I've nursed has ever had a setback and I won't have Mr. McHeath be the first."

"I'll only be a moment," Lady Moira assured her.

Only a moment, but it was more time than he'd had alone with her since that exciting, memorable encounter in the lane.

Mrs. McAlvey nodded and went out, leaving the door open, as was only proper.

Unfortunately, once they were alone, Gordon found it difficult to think clearly, and not because of his injuries. He'd never been so nervous in a woman's presence before. He owed Lady Moira so much, yet all he could think about was kissing her.

Fortunately, she kept a careful distance from the bed. "Is there anything you need?"

You. "No, thank you, my lady. You've already done enough—more than enough."

He was afraid she might leave. He wanted her to stay, even if he could only look at her, to see her lovely, sweet face and the play of light and intelligence and vitality in her eyes.

She didn't leave, and he grasped the opportunity while he had it.

"I'm so sorry I couldn't prevent your school from being destroyed. I shouldn't have investigated on my own. Next time, I'll go back for reinforcements before I attempt any interventions."

"Next time?" she asked, raising a brow as she came a little closer. "First you rescue me from that dog, then you try to stop those vandals single-handedly. Is it your habit to act like a hero?"

He laughed, then winced at the brief spasm of pain that elicited. "Not until I came to Dunbrachie," he said, putting his hand to his side. "Perhaps it's something in the air."

"Or perhaps it's me," she said quietly, looking down at her hands. "I seem to have required a hero since you arrived."

"I'm glad." The words escaped before he thought and he cursed himself for an idiot.

"That is," he amended, "I'm not glad for any trouble that befalls you, my lady, and I would happily prevent any further distress, if I could. I meant that, whatever the circumstances, I'm glad I met you, my lady."

"I wish you wouldn't call me *my lady!*" she said a little peevishly as she turned away and walked toward the window, incidentally giving him a fine view of her profile. She turned back almost at once. "I'm sorry. I'm not used to it, you see. I'm not used to a title, or this house, or...or much of anything here!

"I must sound like an ungrateful wretch," she continued apologetically, "but so much has happened in so short a time." With a sad smile, she started back toward him. "One moment, I was plain Miss MacMurdaugh, daughter of a Glasgow merchant, the next I'm Lady Moira, daughter of the Earl of Dunbrachie."

He was quite sure she had never been *plain* anything.

"I had heard that your father came into the title recently," he replied, not mentioning who had told him.

"We had no idea he was even in line," she admitted, walking toward the bed. "Papa was only distantly related to the previous earl—a third cousin." She spread her hands. "You must just imagine it, Mr. McHeath. Suddenly this huge manor is my home, not our little town house in Glasgow, and we have so many servants and tenants we can hardly remember all their names."

"How long has it been since this change of fortune?"

"A little more than a year, and there are still days I wake up and wonder if I'm dreaming. Or in the middle of a nightmare," she finished grimly, looking down at her feet.

Because of Robbie. And because of *him,* because he had agreed to help his friend bring a legal action against her.

He threw back the covers and, holding his side, cautiously put his feet on the floor.

"What are you doing?" she cried, rushing to his side and putting her arm under his shoulder for support. "You must go back to bed."

"I'm all right," he said, masking the pain, because this was not a conversation he wanted to have lying down. "I don't need any help."

He didn't know if that was true or not, but he didn't want to feel like an invalid when he was with her. Nevertheless, he missed the feel of her body against his as she moved away. She stayed close enough to touch, though.

"I've told Robbie I won't represent him anymore. I can't," he said, putting one hand on the bed to steady himself.

"Because you don't think the suit will succeed?"

"No."

She took a step back. "Because you feel beholden to me?"

"That's one reason."

She flushed, but didn't move away. "Because he might not be able to pay you?"

He felt as if he'd been stabbed again. Did she really think he was that mercenary? And if she did... If she did, he was as wrong about her feelings for him as he'd been about Catriona McNare's. "No, that isn't a factor in my decision."

Her blush deepened. "I'm sorry. I didn't mean to imply... It's just that I've heard something that makes me think he may be having financial difficulties."

Gordon was both relieved and anxious to learn the source of that information. "What did you hear? From whom?"

"Sarah Taggart told me he wants to sell McStuart House. That's why he went to Edinburgh. Why would a man as proud of his heritage as he do that, unless he had to?"

He wanted to be honest with her, and yet...

"Even though I won't be representing Robbie in the future, I can't tell you what he said to me in confidence, either as a friend or a lawyer," he said. "It wouldn't be right, and it wouldn't be ethical."

She frowned and turned away. "Then don't—but I

think Robbie is seriously in debt. I believe that's why he wanted to marry me in the first place, and that's why he's suing me now."

Whatever happened, whether she made him leave at once or let him stay, whether he was right or wrong about her feelings for him, this might be the last chance he had to speak with her alone, and he had to broach one other subject, come what may. "Does your father lose his temper when he's in his cups? Does he strike you?"

She whirled around and stared at him, aghast. "My father has never hit me in his life! He loves me and would never, ever hurt me."

That was good to hear, especially since he was sure she was being truthful. "But he does drink too much, doesn't he?"

Lady Moira drew herself up. "That, sir, is none of your business."

"No, it isn't," he agreed. "I have no right to pry, except that I owe you my life, and anything that hurts or upsets you must therefore concern me. But that isn't the only reason I'm worried about you, my lady, although that would be enough.

"I've seen what drunkenness can do to a family. I've witnessed how men—and women, too—can make their families dance to their tune, as if they're puppets on a string, with promises and guilt, making their lives miserable and uncertain, worrisome and troubled.

"That's another reason you wouldn't marry Robbie, isn't it? It wasn't just the women. You already know what it is to live with a man who drinks too much, and didn't want to have to endure the same trials and worries for the rest of your life."

She met his gaze with admirable steadiness. "Yes, that was partly why, but it was the women, too. That's something my father has never done. He loved my mother very much and was utterly loyal and devoted to her. He *never* drank to excess while she was alive."

"And since then…?"

"Only when he's upset or distressed. He hasn't had a drink in several weeks."

"But you're worried he's drinking now, aren't you, wherever he is?"

"No. He's away on business. He's written, so…"

Moira couldn't keep up the pretence, not with Gordon McHeath looking at her that way. Yet to admit her fears to a man who was still almost a stranger, no matter how he made her feel… "What makes you think my father drinks too much?"

"If it's true, that's all that matters, not how I found out. Has he promised to stop? More than once? And broken that promise again and again, until you've nearly given up hope—but not quite?"

He knew. However it had happened, he knew what she endured and regarded her with sympathy. "Yes," she whispered, deciding to tell him. To trust him.

"No one ever gets used to having their hopes dashed, my lady."

He spoke so quietly, so sincerely, she was reminded of the words he'd murmured when they'd first brought him here. "Do you still have hope, Mr. McHeath, although your heart was broken?"

He stepped back as if the ground had started to shake. "I beg your pardon?"

"When you were hurt, you spoke of a woman named Catriona, who apparently led you on while caring for another."

When his brows lowered, she said, "You talked about my troubles. Isn't it fair we speak of yours?"

He frowned, but answered nonetheless. "Catriona didn't lead me on. She never said she cared for me in that way. It was only my hope that led me to interpret her responses as more than the affection one might have for a friend."

He could demure all he liked; the pain was there, in his eyes. "Yet your heart was broken just the same."

He shook his head. "Not broken. Wounded, but not broken. I've since discovered that I never really loved her."

Her heart suddenly felt much…lighter.

"What else did I say?" he asked.

"That you came to Dunbrachie to get away. Instead, you've found more trouble, been set upon and almost killed."

"Whatever happened, whatever the future holds for us, my lady, I'll never regret coming to Dunbrachie," he said softly, the sincerity shining in his eyes. "If I hadn't come here, I would never have met a beautiful, spirited young woman hiding in a tree."

He couldn't help it. He had to reach out to take her hand, to feel her skin warm and soft against his own. Now he knew that love wasn't just an attraction born of admiration. He had learned that affection and desire, respect and admiration, could be combined into a devotion that would last a lifetime.

That was how he felt about Moira. It was more than desire, more than affection.

It had to be love.

As that realization crashed into his mind, it was as if everything stopped. The moon and stars in their course, time, the earth on its axis. He couldn't even be sure he was breathing as he drew her to him, his wounds forgotten, aware only of her shining, passionate eyes, her soft lips and the growing need within him that he could no longer ignore.

Or fight.

Chapter Fifteen

$Moira$ had been waiting for his kiss. Dreaming of it, even though she hadn't wanted to admit it. Yet the moment their mouths met, it felt right and good and wonderful.

She leaned forward and responded with an eager, aching need, willingly parting her lips to allow his tongue to venture within and deepening the kiss as desire flowed between them, infusing the very air. His arms around her, his hands roved over her body while she explored his, feeling the warmth of his skin. His shirt the merest of barriers, she could feel the heat of his body, the matching heat of the same impulse that compelled her to stay when she should go, to lean toward him instead of hurrying away, to kiss him and surrender, rather than flee.

With slow deliberation, his right hand slipped around to cup her breast. He kneaded gently, the action increasing her fervent yearning for more. More of his kisses. More of his embrace. More intimacy.

She moved closer, trying to get as near to him as possible, grasping him tighter until she felt his body stiffen and the sharp intake of his breath.

The wound in his side. She had forgotten and put her arm around him, and the bandage there.

At once she pulled away. "I'm sorry. I don't want to hurt you," she whispered.

He smiled and caressed her cheek. "If I'm in any pain, it's not because of anything you're doing, and certainly not enough to ask you to stop."

She didn't want to hurt him in *any* way, not like that other woman. Nor did she want her own heart to suffer more than it would when he left Dunbrachie, so she took another step backward. "I should let you rest."

Before he could answer, a voice shouted from the foyer, "Moira! Where the devil are you?"

"Papa!" she gasped. "He's back! I should go to him."

"I'll go with you," Gordon said, holding her hand.

"No!" she exclaimed. "Let me tell him about what happened first. It will be better that way."

He wanted to protest, to protect her, except that he had no right to. And she had shown him that she was capable of protecting herself and making her own decisions.

"Saints preserve me!" Mrs. McAlvey cried as she bustled into the room carrying a tray with covered dishes on it. "I assume that's your father, my lady, and if he is, be careful. He looks angry enough to spit tacks!"

He must have learned Mr. McHeath was there.

The longer she took, the angrier her father might get, so with a final encouraging smile from Gordon, Moira hurried out of the room and down the stairs toward her father.

He stood in the middle of the foyer, hands on his hips, scowling. Walters and two footmen waited nearby, both of them looking equally ill at ease.

Worse than that, her father's clothes were soiled and dishevelled and his eyes were bloodshot. Worst of all, the closer she got to him, the more she could smell the wine.

She took a deep breath. *Be calm,* she ordered herself. *For his sake and yours, be calm.*

"There you are!" the earl exclaimed when he saw her, his accent betraying more of his impoverished youth in Glasgow than usual, providing further proof that he had weakened and once again had too much to drink.

"Moira, you're safe!" he cried, and she was taken aback to realize he was nearly in tears as he enveloped her in a hug. "They told me about the fire when I stopped at the inn. I saw the school. Are you all right?"

"I'm fine. The fire happened at night, so I was nowhere near it," she said, drawing back, wanting to get him away from the servants and safely in bed. "Would you like to rest? I can explain everything later."

"In a moment. Who was that woman I saw running up the stairs?"

He had to mean Mrs. McAlvey. "I'll explain that later, too," she said, taking his arm to lead him to his room.

Unfortunately, her father could be very stubborn, and

the downturn of his mouth told her he was about to be. "I want to know who's in my house, and why, and I want to know *now!*"

She had learned long ago that it was fruitless to try to dissuade him when he was in such a state. She didn't relish telling him more, but it would be better if he heard everything from her.

"All right, Papa," she said, gently pulling him toward the drawing room. "I'll tell you all about it."

Mercifully, he didn't protest, but followed meekly enough, even sitting when she asked him to.

"I saw the fire from my window," she began without waiting for him to ask a question. "I realized what it was and woke the servants. We went at once, but by the time we got there, the school was already too far gone to save."

"It's totally destroyed?"

"Yes, but that's not all. A man was also attacked by the vandals who set the fire. They stabbed him and left him for dead."

His father blanched. "Good God, Moira!" he cried, leaping to his feet. "It could have been you, Moira, beaten or...or worse. I was afraid of something like this. Have I not warned you that your charitable impulses, however well-meaning, could have unforeseen and dangerous consequences?"

"I wouldn't have been there alone at night, like Mr...." She hesitated. "The man upstairs who tried to go for help to stop the ones who set it—who were paid to do it."

"Paid? How do you know that?" her father demanded incredulously.

"He overheard them talking."

"Who overheard them?"

"The man upstairs."

Her father regarded her warily. "Who is he, Moira?"

She winced inwardly, but there was no help for it. She had to tell him. "Mr. McHeath."

"McHeath?" her father repeated, aghast with both shock and dismay. "*McHeath?* Sir Robert's solicitor? The one who's suing you?"

"Sir Robert's suing me. Mr. McHeath is only the solicitor and—"

"*Only?*" her father charged. "*Only?* You might as well say a demon is *only* in league with the devil!"

"Papa, it's not as bad as that. And he tried to stop whoever set the fire. But even if he hadn't, even if he was Sir Robert's solicitor, surely it is good and right to offer help to *anyone* who needs it."

"I am all for a kind heart in a woman, Moira," her father retorted, "but this is too much. If he's hurt, let him go to Sir Robert—who, you may recall, is suing you for a considerable sum of money."

"Should that really matter if the man is injured? And isn't it possible Robbie misled him, too, the same way he misled me? I gather it's been a few years since Mr. McHeath has seen Robbie. A man can change a good deal in that time."

"Or not," her father countered.

"Whether he has or not, Mr. McHeath is still a man who's been seriously hurt," she replied, her frustration and desperation mounting, for the servants would obey her father's orders over hers, "so much so that the doctor says it's too risky to move him just yet. By letting Mr. McHeath stay here, we're ensuring his recovery, as well we should. Dr. Campbell says—"

"Don't quote a doctor to me! They don't know anything! I want him gone tomorrow. I'll have the footmen carry him out if I have to."

"Unless you're drunk."

The words came out seemingly of their own volition, released like caged tigers that had been waiting, pacing, ready to pounce, for years.

As her father's face reddened, her hand flew to her lips as if to trap them again. "Papa, I'm—"

"Is this how you repay me for all I've given you?" he interrupted, his face going as red as poppies. "All I've done for you? For indulging in these charitable whims of yours about educating the children of people who don't want them to be educated? Did you ever stop to think how your plans affected me, Moira? Has it never occurred to you that your schemes for schools and education might be an embarrassment to me, and even cost me business?"

No, it hadn't.

"Or that your broken engagement has forced me to listen to snide remarks about my unmarriageable daughter with her jilted fiancé and misguided charity.

"All I've ever wanted is your happiness, Moira. To see you married, with a good husband and children around you. Why else do you think I told you what I learned about that devil you were going to marry, while you were blinded by his looks and name and nobility? God,

Moira, I could have let you marry the man and boasted of the connection—aye, and made use of it, too. But I didn't.

"Now I fear you're going to wind up so immersed in your good deeds you'll never get a husband. Is that what you want, Moira? To be an old maid? To be the sort of woman everyone admires and no man will wed?"

She clasped her hands as she fought to find the words to make him understand. "Papa, can't you see that I'm trying to make something of myself, as you did when you were a young man? I want to leave something built of hard work and effort, the same way you made your fortune.

"Yes, you gave me a fine home and good clothes, but you also gave me fear and worry and heartache. How many times have you come home stinking of drink and I had to put you to bed, Papa? How many times have you stayed out until all hours, and I never knew where you were? Or if you were well, or lying in some gutter? How many nights have I lost sleep waiting for you to come home after a night of drinking, when I didn't know where you were or even if you would come home?

"I want to be proud of you, Papa, not ashamed, and I'll be ashamed—and more—if you make Mr. McHeath leave before the doctor thinks it's safe. Please don't rob me of the pride I should feel for my father, who did work and slave and make something of himself before he fell into a title."

Her father's expression didn't soften so much as alter to one that she recognized—the same one he wore when he was bargaining with a tradesman. "I'm not completely heartless, Moira. I'll agree to let him stay until the doctor says he is well enough to be taken to Sir Robert's—on the condition that you never again try to open a school in Dunbrachie."

She gasped. "How can you give me such an ultimatum? I've only ever asked three things of you—that you stop drinking to excess, that you provide the funds to let me open a school and that Mr. McHeath stay here until he's well. You've broken your promise about the first more than once, and now you ask me to give up my school or you'll send an injured man from our home? How can you, Papa? Is that fair? Is it just? Is it kind?"

"I won't discuss this anymore, Moira," he said, walking to the door. "If you want Mr. McHeath to stay, he may—but you won't get another penny for a school in Dunbrachie, or anywhere else, if he does."

She could hardly believe her ears, but she knew him too well to doubt that he meant what he said. Yet she was also her father's daughter, and that meant that she could be just as resolute. She must be now, for Lillibet and the other children of Dunbrachie.

"Mr. McHeath is going to stay until the doctor says he's well enough to leave," she said, marching to the door, "and I *will* build a school in Dunbrachie. If you won't help me, I'll find the money for it somewhere else."

Too upset to see or speak to anyone, Moira sought sanctuary in her morning room.

What was she going to do? She had to build her school. It had been her dream for a long time, and

Lillibet and all the other children deserved the opportunity of education.

Surely she could raise the money herself…in Glasgow, where she had so many friends. Not Edinburgh, where she didn't know a soul except Robbie and Gordon McHeath. She really would have no reason to go there….

A shadow fell across the carpet and she swiped at her tear-filled eyes before she turned to find Walters on the threshold.

"I beg your pardon, my lady," the butler said, "but the earl has asked me to inform you that he's left for Glasgow."

She shouldn't be surprised he hadn't stayed, not after that quarrel and their mutual accusations. "Did he say when he would return?"

"No, my lady. He merely left orders that Mr. McHeath was to leave as soon as the doctor said he could."

Her father had left no word for her? Given how they'd parted, perhaps she shouldn't be surprised by that, either. "I see. Thank you."

The butler nodded and she walked toward the window that overlooked the garden.

Another shadow fell upon the wall beside her. Perhaps her father had left some word for her with the footman or another servant, she thought, turning.

It wasn't a servant. It was Gordon McHeath.

Chapter Sixteen

He was dressed in his trousers that had been cleaned
and pressed, his polished boots and a plain shirt that
must belong to one of the servants. It looked as if he
were leaving.

But he shouldn't even be on his feet.

"Mr. McHeath!" she cried, hurrying to him. "You
shouldn't be out of bed! Please, sit down. I'm shocked
Mrs. McAlvey let you come downstairs."

"I wanted to make sure you're all right—and Mrs.
McAlvey doesn't know I'm not in bed." He flushed as
he gave her a little smile and she helped him to the
sofa. "She's getting me some biscuits and tea. I told her
I was famished. Never mind how I'm feeling. How are
you?"

"I'm all right." Since he already knew about her
father's drinking, she could meet his steadfast gaze as
she sat beside him. In spite of her shame over her father's

reaction to his presence, it was a relief not to have to prevaricate. "I think Papa's been drinking again. He worries about me, so when he found out about the fire and that you were here…"

"He was justifiably upset that the solicitor who was helping Sir Robert to sue you has been your guest," he said with both acceptance and resignation. "Regardless of what Dr. Campbell says, it would probably be best if I left today, if I may borrow a carriage. I can stay in the village for a night or two, and Mrs. McAlvey can come with me."

She wanted to go with him, but of course that was impossible. Equally impossible, however, was letting him leave before the doctor said he should. "My father will get over his anger." *Eventually.* "So you mustn't even think of leaving until Dr. Campbell says you may."

"I don't want to make things worse for you than I already have. Your father was angry enough to shout, Moira. My presence will cause trouble for you if I stay, so I won't."

Toying with the cuff of the narrow sleeve of her gown, Moira looked up into his face. "If my life is troubled now, it's not your fault. You were just the catalyst that led to revelations of things I should know. Now that I'm aware of how vindictive Robert McStuart is, I can take precautions to avoid him, and men like him, in the future. It's also better that I discover my father's true feelings about my plans and goals. He's never been overjoyed by my endeavors, but I didn't realize how much he was against the school. When he found out I planned to rebuild, he withdrew his support. If I wish to build the school again, I shall have to find the money myself—and I shall."

Gordon had been dazzled by her beauty and impressed by her bravery the first day he met her. He'd come to respect her kindness and generosity. But never had he admired her more than when she spoke of rebuilding the school with such heartfelt resolve. "I'm so sorry, Moira," he said softly. "I should have insisted on leaving at once."

"And put yourself at even more risk? No, Mr. McHeath, you suffered enough. It's not your fault Papa doesn't approve of the school, and if anyone is responsible for the withdrawal of his support, it's whoever set the fire. I shall simply have to solicit donations from my friends. There are many in Glasgow who will surely contribute. I shall go there immediately, and begin."

Glasgow. On the other side of Scotland from Edinburgh. "Have you no friends in Edinburgh?"

She shook her head. "No."

"Except me," he offered, his voice hushed. "I'd be happy to help."

"I should have guessed you would offer," she said. She reached up to cup his cheek, her palm warm and soft against his skin. "You've proven to me that there are good, decent, honorable men in the world."

"Then your experience with Robbie hasn't soured you on men entirely?" he asked, his mind filling with a vision of the future that had been dancing on the edge of his consciousness, yet kept firmly on the fringes.

"Not entirely," she said, lowering her hand, her eyes downcast, her cheeks pink with a blush.

Once before he had kept his feelings to himself, only to discover that he'd been harboring hopes that should never have been allowed to develop. If that was so this time, he had to find out. "Although these are hardly the circumstances I would have wished for, I cannot remain silent any longer about…"

In spite of his determination, his voice faltered. Yet if he were wrong, it would be worse than foolish to remain in ignorance. "About what is happening between us."

She flushed and although she didn't speak, he found her silence encouraging. If he were completely wrong, surely she would say something. "I hope I'm not wrong and that you do feel something more than affection for me," he ventured.

Still she remained silent, red-faced, not meeting his gaze.

His former confidence in her silent response began to ebb away, replaced by dread. Was he wrong again? Perhaps, despite her response to his kisses and embraces, she didn't feel as he did. Maybe his confession was even…embarrassing…to her?

"I had assumed you felt somewhat more," he said. "Apparently, I was mistaken."

She raised her eyes to look at him and in that instant, he knew, to the core of his heart and with the rekindling of all his self-suppressed hopes, that she hadn't been toying with him, or leading him on. "No, Mr. McHeath, you are not mistaken," she said. "Affection is much too weak a word for what I feel for you."

"Not Mr. McHeath. Gordon," he whispered, his heart soaring as he gently took her face between his hands and brought her close to kiss. Lightly, tenderly, he brushed his lips over hers as she closed her eyes and put her arms around him.

"Gordon," she sighed before she kissed him with more fervor, angling her body closer.

Passion leaped into searing, vibrant life within him. His desire liberated, he held her in his arms, where she belonged. Where she would always belong. Where no other woman would have belonged in quite the same perfect way.

She was his equal, in intelligence, in drive, in desire. Having met her, he was completely certain he would never have been happy with a more soft-spoken, timid woman like Catriona McNare.

As if to confirm his thoughts, she parted her lips and his tongue slid between them into her warm, willing mouth. With a low, eager moan, she slid her hands up his back.

He moved to bring himself even closer, ignoring the growing pain in his side from his wound. It was healing, after all. He wouldn't bleed again. Not now, when he had Moira in his arms. Beautiful, determined, passionate Moira.

Warm, wonderful, softly curved Moira.

His hand slowly glided up her side and around to her breast. He could feel the taut tip beneath his fingers and her growing excitement as he brushed the pad of his thumb across it, a match for his own burgeoning need. He shifted and moved her backward, until she was reclining on the sofa and he was half-atop her.

With more of their bodies closer, their kisses grew less tender and more ardent, less gentle and more passionate, as their need increased. He was hard and anxious, his body urging him to take her then and there.

She would let him, he was sure. She wanted him as much as he wanted her, his physical instincts argued. Yet another part of him, the one that was well aware of society's rules, held him in check.

That restraining conscience grew weaker and weaker the more she held and kissed him. The more she moved and arched, as if her body was ordering him to make love with her.

And oh, how much he wanted to! Never had he wanted a woman as much as Moira.

But not like this. Not like some lascivious Casanova, without words of promise and commitment, no matter how difficult it was to stop. To move back. To look down at her flushed face, her desire-darkened eyes, her breasts rising and falling with her rapid breathing, and let go.

She sat up at once, dread in her lovely eyes. "Are you bleeding again?"

He shook his head. "No. It's not that. This isn't… right," he said, the words so difficult to say, but necessary.

Her brows contracting with a frown, she straightened and tucked a stray lock of hair behind her ear. "I realize this sort of thing is highly inappropriate."

Oh, God, he'd offended her, and that was the last thing he wanted to do. He reached out and took hold of her hand. "Moira, I'm not sorry I kissed you, here or any other time. And I want to be with you, intimately and every other way. But we have to stop, or we are going to make love right here on this sofa. As delightful as making love with you would be, I won't take you like some lascivious Lothario, the way Robbie—"

"He didn't."

The words burst out of her like cannon fire as she swiftly rose. "We didn't. Never. I've never behaved like this with any man. I don't know what comes over me when I'm with you!"

She was upset, and yet she had no reason to be. Putting a hand on the back of the sofa, he hoisted himself to his feet. "I wasn't accusing you of anything. As for what comes over you when we're together, it's the same thing that comes over me, because I assure you, Moira, I have never been so presumptuous in my life."

"Presumptuous?" she repeated, and he was glad to see the spark of anger shift to a sparkle of amusement. "Is that what you call it?"

He put his arms about her waist and smiled. "I suppose I could call it brazen desire. Audacious need. Bold passion."

She raised herself on her toes and lightly touched her lips to his. "I call it daring. Passionate. Exciting."

"Quite the last words one expects to hear used to describe a solicitor."

"Yet appropriate in this case." She ran her fingertip along the bandage that covered the gash over his eye. "Mrs. McAlvey thinks you're going to have a scar.

You'll look even more daring then. I daresay you'll have widows flocking to your office."

"There's only one person I want anxious to see me," he murmured as he bent his head to kiss her again. "The same woman who would climb on a rooftop to watch a prizefight."

"You saw me?"

"Aye. I was quite astonished."

"You weren't distracted?"

"Only for a moment—and I'm not sorry a bit. However did you get up there?"

"I told you—I used to climb in my father's warehouses. I wanted to watch, but of course a lady shouldn't, so…"

"So you found a way, despite society's conventions."

"The way I disobey society's conventions when I'm with you," she said with a disarming smile.

How could he resist? He had to bring her back into the circle of his arms. He had to kiss her again and was leaning down to do so when Mrs. McAlvey charged into the room.

"What on earth?!" the nurse cried as they jumped apart like guilty children caught stealing cake. "Tea and scones my right hind foot!"

Mrs. McAlvey came to a halt and waggled her finger. "I trusted you, Mr. McHeath, but when I go back upstairs, what do I find? Or *not* find? You're down here! I thought you'd have more sense! If that wound's opened again, I've a good mind to let you bleed to death!"

In spite of her annoyance and just condemnation for disobeying orders, Gordon was only a little embarrassed;

he was much too happy to learn that Moira cared for him to be dismayed. Moira blushed, but otherwise didn't look any more contrite.

He reached under his shirt and felt his bandage. "Dry as a bone, Mrs. McAlvey, so no need to fuss," he said, although the wound was sore. "I did want some tea and scones, but I was feeling so well that I—"

"Thought you knew better than the doctor and me?" Her hands on her hips, she turned to address Moira. "If he didn't have more sense, you should have, my lady. You should have sent him back upstairs at once."

"I'm sorry," she replied, managing to sound remorseful in spite of the happiness lurking in her eyes and the corners of her mouth.

How much he wanted to kiss her there! And on the tip of her delightful nose. And the soft lobes of her ears. The curve of her cheek.

The curve of her breast…

"I don't know what I'm going to do with you—the pair of you!" Mrs. McAlvey declared as she took hold of Gordon's arm as if he were an escaped convict. "Now back to bed, you stupid man, before I send to the doctor for something that'll make you sleep for a week."

"Yes, Mrs. McAlvey. I'll do whatever you say, Mrs. McAlvey."

"You should," Moira agreed, "since you have to stay a few more days."

"Yes, my lady," he said, looking back at her over his shoulder, and giving her a saucy wink that was so unsolicitor-like, she had to laugh as she sat on the sofa and covered her warm cheeks with her hands.

In an instant, everything had changed. There was still her conflict with her father, and her school to be rebuilt, but knowing Gordon cared so much for her made her feel that the worst was over.

She would reconcile with her father. She would rebuild her school. She would have Gordon, and all would be well.

Even the dog was miserable as master and beast huddled in the narrow cave.

"How's he goin' t' know where t' find us?" Charlie grumbled as he stroked the head of his dog. "We're nowhere near the meeting place."

"We're closer than you think," Red replied as he crawled forward on his belly to look into the band of trees that covered the slope. They were about five miles from Dunbrachie, where the ground was more uneven and the river in more of a valley. He could see parts of it through the trees and the slight drizzle that added to their discomfort. "He himself told me where t' go if I thought we had t' hide better."

"That other place was warmer. At least there was straw."

"Aye, but we couldn't stay there. Not after that dolt fell and killed himself."

"Then why'd we go t' all the trouble to move him? I thought we done that so we could stay where we was."

"Too close for comfort." Red shivered and muttered a sailor's curse. "By God, he's going to have to pay for keeping us waiting in this hole like worms."

Charlie scratched one of the fleabites on his arm. "If

he comes at all. It's been too long, I tells ya. He ain't comin' a'tall. We been cheated. We done what he said, put our necks in the noose and all for naught."

Red glared at him over his shoulder. "Shut yer gob."

Charlie's dog rose, growling.

With a triumphant grunt, Red raised himself on his elbows, then scrambled up on his hands and knees. "Here he comes! I told you he'd come!"

Red moved back from the opening and sat on his haunches, satisfaction on his face. "I told you!"

"Is he by himself?"

"Aye." Red rose, standing as straight as he could beneath the overhang.

"What if he ain't? I say let him come up here, not us go down where we'll be seen."

Red hesitated for the briefest of moments before shaking his head. "He won't be able to make it up the slope," he said as he went to the entrance and started to climb out.

"Stupid git," Charlie muttered. "Go on, Dan," he ordered his dog, who leaped eagerly out of the cave.

Charlie followed more slowly, his gaze sweeping over the slope, the bushes, the rocky riverbank and the scattered, stunted trees.

Below him Red lumbered down the slope like a bear, heading toward the well-dressed fellow waiting near a spruce that likely wouldn't last another winter. The man appeared to be alone, but there could be other men hidden nearby, with guns and ropes to bind them. Then it would be prison and the hangman's noose.

Maybe he should cut and run right now. Let Red be caught and imprisoned.

But what if the man was alone and intending to pay? He had less than a shilling in his pocket, and no food at all.

Hungry, uncertain, wishing he'd stayed in Glasgow, Charlie watched as Red approached the nobleman. He saw his confederate's shoulders relax, and then the nobleman brought out a purse.

He'd brought the payment after all.

Whistling for Dan, wanting to keep his dog beside him because it could still be a trap, Charlie hurried down the slope.

But when he got there, the earl was still holding tight to the money, his voice raised in anger.

"All you were supposed to do was frighten my daughter and burn down the building," the old man snarled. "You weren't supposed to hurt anyone. I wanted to prevent violence, not cause it!"

"It wasn't our fault that fella came along when he did," Red protested. "And what else should we have done? Let him walk away? Told 'im you were payin' for the job?"

"If it was already alight, you should have fled."

"It wasn't yet, and he'd seen us. And we ain't been paid. We weren't going anywhere without our money, so it's your fault we had to kill 'em. If you paid us before like I asked—"

"I never pay in full for a job until it's completed to my satisfaction," the earl retorted. "And you *didn't* kill him, you oaf. He's alive and in my house at this very moment."

Charlie and Red both stared at him. "Wha'?" Red muttered. "He ain't dead? But I stabbed him."

"Not deeply enough, apparently, and he can identify you, so I suggest you take this money and go far away—America would probably be best. Nobody cares who goes there," the earl growled as he finally shoved the leather purse into Red's hand.

Scowling, Red weighed the pouch in his hand. "There ain't enough here for both of us to sail for America. And you kept us here when we could ha' been well away. More risk for us, more it'll cost ya—another fifty pound or so."

"Are you daft?" the earl demanded.

"No, my lord. We're willin' to go far away if you're willin' to pay. O' course, if you're not, we could always ask your pretty daughter for more. Don't you think she'd pay us, Charlie, rather than have everybody in Dunbrachie know what her father done?"

Blanching, the earl drew a pistol from his greatcoat. "I could shoot you down like rabid dogs and all I'd have to say is that you tried to rob me."

Charlie glanced at his dog, sitting obediently at his side. All *he* had to do was whisper a word and Dan would attack, as ferocious as a lion.

"If you attempt to talk to my daughter—if she so much as sees you from a distance—you'll be sorry. If you're caught, you'll hang. And if you try to involve me, there's not a soul in Scotland who'll believe your word over mine. After all, why would I want to destroy my own daughter's school?"

"Maybe your daughter isn't as stupid as you think," Red replied. "Might be she'll believe us. After all, why else would we come to this godforsaken place? Not for the sport of it, that's for sure. And she's heard of the Three Feathers in Glasgow, ain't she? If we say that's where we met you, she'll believe it, won't she? Ain't she had to send servants to drag you out o' there often enough?"

Charlie kept his eyes on the earl. He'd worked with mute beasts long enough to recognize a silent human reaction, and the man hesitated a moment too long before saying, "You can make all the accusations you like. My daughter will never believe you."

Whatever he said, the earl had doubts about his daughter's trust in him.

They had him. They had him good. "I'm thinkin' we ought to get more than fifty," Charlie said. "After all, we'll hang if we're caught, whether we got a hundred pounds or twenty. Might as well get a hundred. We can go back to that empty barn at the edge of your grounds, my lord. That's convenient for ya, ain't it?"

"I don't have a hundred pounds in ready money!" the earl protested.

"But you can get it," Charlie amiably replied. "And you'd better, or your daughter'll be finding out just what kind o' man her pa is."

"How?" he charged, panic in his voice. "You wouldn't dare show your face in Dunbrachie!"

"Your house ain't in Dunbrachie, and there ain't a lock in Scotland Charlie here can't pick," Red noted with a smirk. "If we want to pay a little visit during the night, we can. And, by God, we will."

Chapter Seventeen

Embarrassed but determined, Moira clutched her reticule as she declined the offer of a chair after she entered Mr. Stamford's parlor. The room wasn't large but had many cunningly contrived shelves and cupboards, and the pine boards of the floor had been very well laid. The mantel was strong and yet lovely to look at, like the Dutch tiles around it. The expert construction and finishing of his home had been one reason she'd hired him to build her school. The furnishings were plain and likewise well made, reminding her of their home in Glasgow.

Taking a deep breath, Moira got right to the point. "I'm very sorry, Mr. Stamford, but my father has declined to pay for the rebuilding of the school. That will have to wait until I can raise the funds myself." She reached into her reticule and pulled out a cheque for nearly the whole amount of her remaining pin money, except for enough to get her to Glasgow, where she could stay with friends. On the other side of country from Edinburgh. "In the meantime, this should be sufficient to cover your costs thus far."

Mr. Stamford took the cheque with surprising delicacy. "We've had our differences, my lady, but I'm sorry it's come to this. You're sure your father won't change his mind?"

"No. After the fire and the attack on Mr. McHeath, he thinks what I'm trying to do is too dangerous. I don't agree, so he's withdrawn his support completely."

Mr. Stamford tapped his chin with the cheque. "I can't say I blame him, my lady. I might do the same if you were my daughter."

"Things have come to a sad pass if vandals get their way, Mr. Stamford, and I don't intend for that to happen," Moira said as she made her way to the door. "While I regret having to call a temporary halt to our project, I have every confidence that it *is* temporary, and I hope you'll be available when I have the necessary funds to begin again."

"Yes, my lady, you can count on me. How is the young solicitor? A terrible business, that."

"Doing much better, I'm happy to say." Better enough to come downstairs. Better enough to kiss her and almost make love with her.

Better enough that surely the doctor would say he was well enough to go home.

And then what? And then what? Those words had been a refrain in her mind all last night and this morning, and all the way into Dunbrachie.

"I'm glad to hear it. I never saw such a prizefight in all my life."

Neither had she, but then, she'd never seen any kind of prizefight and never wanted to see another. "Good day, Mr. Stamford. I'll let you know when we can begin building the school again."

"Aye, my lady. I'll be waiting."

"I wish I could say you're fit as a fiddle," Dr. Campbell said as he examined the wound in Gordon's side, "but you'd be a little out of tune. Mrs. McAlvey tells me you've been doing more than you ought, so I can't say I'm surprised."

Gordon darted a swift glance at the nurse, who was standing at the foot of the bed with the virtuous expression of an angel. "Has she indeed?"

"It's my duty to tell the doctor you didn't stay in bed," she said, as calm and gentle as a nun.

Gordon wondered if that was all she'd told him, and he got his answer when she winked at him behind the doctor's back.

He was glad she'd been reticent on exactly what he'd been doing, but he blushed nonetheless.

The doctor immediately put his hand on Gordon's forehead.

"Is that a fever or are you rightly ashamed of yourself for disobeying your doctor's orders?"

"I'm sorry I didn't do as I was told," Gordon contritely replied, "but it's difficult to stay in bed when you don't feel sick."

"Well, no serious harm done, it seems," Dr. Campbell

said as he began to rebandage Gordon's torso. "This is healing quite nicely, really. I see no reason you can't go home today or tomorrow, if your carriage goes at a moderate pace."

Gordon had a reason not to go home, and it had nothing to do with the speed of the journey. However, he did have clients waiting, and he could hardly abandon them, at least so abruptly. Perhaps in time, gradually, he could move his legal business to Glasgow.

But that was in the future. For now, he had to go back to Edinburgh. "I didn't come in a carriage. I suppose I can hire one in the village?"

"Aye, at the livery," the doctor answered. "And a driver, too. I recommend no more than ten miles a day. It'll take you longer, but you'll be the better for it."

"Thank you, Doctor, and remember what I said about the bill."

Dr. Campbell nodded as they shook hands. "Good day, and good luck, Mr. McHeath," he said, then turned and left the room.

"I'll be leaving now, too," Mrs. McAlvey announced. "You don't need a nurse anymore—not that you listened to me anyway."

"I'm very grateful for all that you've done for me, and you'll find an appropriate expression when I send a cheque for your services," Gordon said. "I'm sure I wouldn't have recovered so well without you."

Her lips curved into a sly little smile. "Oh, I think you would have. I don't think it was me that made you mend so fast. Nothing like love's promise to make a person get better."

He considered protesting, but how could he, when she'd seen him with Moira in the morning room?

"And I trust you won't do any more prizefighting," she said sternly. "Such carryings-on for a grown man, and a solicitor, too!"

"That was my last fight, I assure you."

"Good. You'll break that poor girl's heart if you get hurt again, and she's got enough to worry about with that father of hers." Her brow furrowed as she patted him on the arm. "I suppose I ought to warn you. Although they're on the outs for now, she's too used to taking care of him to ever really stop."

He wouldn't expect anything else. "No, I don't think she ever will."

"Well, as long as you know what you're in for," she said as she picked up her valise, which he hadn't seen behind the door.

"She's worth it, Mrs. McAlvey. More than worth it."

The nurse gave him a warm smile. "Aye, I suppose she is. Well, sir, I wish you all the best, and Lady Moira, too."

He held out his hand. "Goodbye, Mrs. McAlvey, and thank you."

Instead of taking it, she enfolded him in her arms. "You take care. And marry that girl."

That was easy enough for Mrs. McAlvey to say, Gordon reflected after she had gone and he was alone. He'd like nothing better than to marry Lady Moira.

However, in his business he was used to considering

cold, hard facts in the bright light of day, and he did so now, trying to keep his feelings—his need, his desire—out of it.

She was a lady; he was just a lawyer.

Her father considered him an enemy, and he—Gordon—was responsible for a breach between father and daughter that might continue for months or even years, and would be painful for them both.

Moira had her school to build; he had his clients.

She would be in Glasgow; he would be in Edinburgh.

Most importantly of all, could either of them really trust their emotions? Once before he thought he was in love; she had believed she loved Robbie. How could either of them be sure that what they felt was truly a love that would last the rest of their lives unless they spent more time together?

Yet they had no more time, for tomorrow, he would go to Edinburgh and she would not.

Dressed in her nightgown, bedrobe and slippers, Moira crept quietly along the corridor toward the blue bedroom sometime after midnight. Tomorrow morning, Gordon McHeath was leaving for Edinburgh and she was determined to see him alone before he departed, just as he had been firm in his decision to go when they spoke at dinner, and afterward, when they'd sat on opposite sides of the hearth, careful not to get too close, lest the butler or maid come to the door.

She, too, was still resolved to go to Glasgow to raise money for her school, so much so, anybody overhearing would have thought they were having a calm, rational discussion of their future plans, and that they would likely never see each other again.

In reality, it hadn't been like that at all. Underneath their serene, deliberate words had been that smoldering desire waiting for release, that same deep affection and respect.

That feeling that had to be love.

There was light coming from beneath the door of the blue bedroom, telling her Gordon was still awake. Because a young unmarried woman shouldn't be alone with an unmarried man at this time of night, she didn't knock before she opened his door and slipped inside.

Gordon stood by the hearth, one hand on the mantel as he stared into the flames. He hadn't disrobed; he wore the same clothes he'd had on before—dark trousers, white shirt and riding boots. He had taken off his cravat and loosened his collar, but that was all.

The only light came from that low fire. Everything else, including the bed, was in shadow, so that it looked as if he were marooned there, and waiting to be rescued.

"Gordon," she whispered, venturing farther inside.

"Moira!" he cried softly, straightening, his brow furrowing as he ran his gaze over her, making her warm despite the thinness of the fabric, and her nipples harden as if he had touched them. "What are you doing here? You should go. If anybody finds you here—"

"I realize this isn't proper," she said, "but I couldn't let you go without seeing you once more, in private."

Where they wouldn't be interrupted. Where they could be alone, together.

As she came closer, his body grew more tense, his gaze more searching, as if he couldn't quite understand.

"Tomorrow, you go to Edinburgh and I'll be going to Glasgow in a few days," she began, "and I didn't want to leave without saying...without telling you..."

Now that the time had come to say the words, her confidence seemed to have disappeared along with his cravat.

His expression softened. "What is it, Moira?" he asked, still keeping his distance, as if he were afraid of what might happen if they got too close, as she ought to be, but wasn't. "What did you want to tell me?"

"I love you," she whispered, the words so simple, yet so potent. Words she had never said to Robbie.

His eyes shone in the firelight and his lips curved into a smile. Finally, he moved away from the mantel toward her.

"Moira, my darling, I love you, too," he said as he met her in the middle of the room and took her hands in his. "I care about you more than any other woman I've ever met. I love you more than I ever guessed it was possible to love anyone. I hardly dared to hope you could ever love me, yet my feelings were so strong...right from the moment I met you."

"Mine, too. From the moment I saw you running down the hill to help me, like Galahad."

"Hardly a Galahad. I stumbled."

"Yet you recovered so gracefully," she murmured as she lifted her face for his kiss.

No wonder they'd kept their distance here, and in the dining room, because the instant their lips met, their passionate desire exploded. His mouth took hers, hard and strong. She returned his passion, measure for measure.

This heated kiss, this intense embrace, was as different from the others as a grown man was from a boy.

As she was no girl, but a woman, and a woman willing and wanting, eager and excited, thrilled by the power of his need that equalled her own.

"Marry me, Moira," he said as his lips left hers to trail across her cheek and down the line of her jaw, while his hands continued to caress and stroke her. "Please, marry me. Nothing would make me happier than to spend the rest of my life with you. Moira, please say yes."

She wanted to—oh, how she wanted to! Yet once before she had agreed to marry, and that had been disastrous.

Gordon drew back, his gaze searching her face as she tried to think, to separate the yearning from practicalities, the reality from the beautiful dream. "My school," she said quietly, still holding on to him, not willing to let go. "What about my school? And your practice?"

He ran the tip of his finger along the curve of her jaw. "I know how much the school means to you, so I would never try to stop you from building it. As for my practice, there are plenty of lawyers in Edinburgh. One less will make little difference, and perhaps Dunbrachie could use a new one."

"There aren't any solicitors in Dunbrachie."

That practical observation brought a smile to his face. "Then, my dear, my darling, as soon as I can see that all my current clients have new solicitors, I'll pack my books and bags and return."

"You would give up your practice in Edinburgh for me?"

"I'd do much more than that," he assured her as he bent his head for another deep, soul-searing kiss.

Confident in his love, she returned it eagerly, wantonly, untying the sash of her robe and letting it fall unheeded to the ground as she leaned her body into his. Knowing that he loved her, certain that she loved him, all restraint fell away and she gave herself up to the desire that had been too long denied.

Until he broke the kiss and drew back, panting, and a pang of dismay caught her. "Did I hurt you?" she asked anxiously, for in her selfish need, she'd forgotten about his wounds.

He shook his head. "It's not that," he huskily replied. "We aren't married yet, so I should behave with honor and make you go."

She heard his words, but his body and his eyes told her something else. And she paid more heed to them, as well as the yearning of her own heart. "Tomorrow you'll be going back to Edinburgh, and I must go to Glasgow to raise money for my school. It may be weeks or months before we see each other again. I want you to be sure of me before you go, Gordon. To prove to you that I won't change my mind. I want you to believe that I can and will be constant."

He started to speak, but she pressed her fingertip to

his warm lips. "I want to show you that I believe you when you say you love me. I want to show you how much I love you."

"Moira, I do believe you. There's no need for further proof."

She slid her hands down his long, strong arms. "I think there is. I want there to be," she whispered. "Gordon, please," she murmured, pressing her anxious, nearly naked body against his. "Please, make love with me."

Chapter Eighteen

At first, Gordon didn't respond, as if he was weighing the evidence in his mind, and she feared she had finally stepped over the mark, been too brazen and gone too far.

But then…oh, then!

It was as if the vessel holding his desire shattered, to release the emotions bottled within. He took her in his arms and kissed her with such passion, she could scarcely breathe.

She didn't care if she never breathed again, as long as he let her stay with him and kept kissing her. As long as he wanted her with such fierce yearning, a longing that quickly engulfed and enflamed her, too.

For one brief instant, she realized that she had never felt anything even close to this overwhelming physical need for a man. Never in her life had she wanted to know every inch of a man's body, and to have him as familiar with hers. To kiss and stroke and caress, to lick and touch and graze.

With fervent hunger to do all that and more, she broke the kiss to undo the remaining buttons of his shirt. She abandoned any pretence of maidenly modesty as she lost her patience. She tore off the buttons in her haste before capturing his mouth again. She shoved his shirt aside to slide her hands over his hot, naked chest above the bandage still wrapped around his torso.

Then, oh, then! He swept her up in his strong arms and carried her to the bed, setting her down as gently as if she were made of delicate glass.

But as he stepped back and tugged off his shirt, his eyes told a different story—that he was looking at a woman, and one he wanted as much as any man, civilized or primitive, had ever wanted a woman. That his whole being was concentrated on assuaging a physical need as powerful as the one coursing through her body.

Just as quickly his boots were off and then his trousers, until he was completely naked except for the wide swath of linen around his middle. The rest of him was bruised, battered, and beautifully nude.

Powerfully, primitively ready to love her.

With a last mental gasp, modesty and the strictures of society reared up in her mind, a distant shout of wary caution that once she let this man possess her, there would be no going back. Her maidenhood, once gone, could never be retrieved.

That what she was giving up, giving to him, was something she could only give to him, and no one else.

Her flash of doubt, her moment's hesitation, must have shown in her face, for his expression changed and he reached for his trousers. "Go," he said softly. "Leave me, Moira."

"No!" she cried, grabbing for his trousers and pulling them from his grasp, her qualms overruled by the need to be with him and to prove to him how sincere she was. "I don't want to go. I want to stay with you.

"I want to be with you," she said even more firmly as she yanked her nightgown over her head, revealing her body to him.

"I want to love you and for you to love me," she whispered as she reached out to take both his hands and draw him onto the bed with her.

"Please be with me," she said as she brushed the hair from his brow and looked into his smoldering eyes, seeing in them all that she had ever hoped to see in the eyes of a man who loved her. "I want you, Gordon, here and now and forever. I want you to make love with me. I want to make love to you."

Although his body betrayed his animal desire and their bodies were nearly touching, he didn't act. "Moira, you don't have to prove yourself to me in this way. I believe that you love me. I believe that you'll be true to me, even if we have to be apart for a time."

He meant it; it was plain in his face. And she was sure he would be true to her, no matter how long they had to be away from each other. She also trusted her own feelings, confident that what she felt for Gordon McHeath was no fleeting fancy, no shallow emotion based on flattery and pride. She had faith that she could rise from this bed right now without another kiss or caress, and they would still be married one day, their union lawful and free of the risk of scandal. He didn't need to possess her body to know he had her heart.

So the only reason to be with him here and now was…because she wanted to be.

And oh, how she wanted to be! "I believe you, Gordon. I trust you. And if you really want me to leave, I will go—but only because you ask me. Otherwise, I'll stay, because I want to be with you tonight, Gordon. I want to love you and have you love me. I want something good to remember if things get difficult in the coming days. I want to remember what it's like to hold you in my arms, to be yours in every way, until we can be married. Will you give me that, Gordon? Will you let me stay and make love with me?"

"I haven't the strength to refuse. I love you so much and I want you too much," he whispered as he gazed down at her.

He bent down and his lips covered hers with a gentler kiss, a touch of tenderness and promise. A demonstration of the kind of devotion they would share once the fiercer passion was spent.

With gentle yet insistent pressure he moved his mouth over hers and insinuated his tongue between her parted lips. Her body relaxed, and she felt free of worry and care.

As his tongue slipped into her mouth, he shifted until

his hips were between her thighs. She slid her hands over the plane of his back, across the brief expanse of the bandage and over the contours of his buttocks. His body was like a new country whose terrain she wanted to learn and explore, as she had once explored this house. Except that he was much more interesting.

As he leaned his weight on his left elbow, his right hand grazed with agonizing leisure over her body, from the curve of her collarbone over the roundness of her breast and the ridges of her ribs, across her taut belly and lower still.

As their lips and tongues moved in a sinuous dance, she reached up to glide her palm across the breadth of his shoulders, aware of the muscles beneath the hot flesh, the tense sinews and smooth skin.

He broke the kiss, licking the edge of her jaw, then the lobe of her ear. Like a dancer stretching, she arched her back as his hand crept up again to knead her breast. But he did more than touch and stroke. She gasped with surprise and arousal when he sucked her pebbled nipple into his mouth, then groaned with exquisitely tense agony as he circled the tip with his tongue. He continued to lick and tongue and tease until she squirmed beneath him, breathlessly, wordlessly, urging him on.

Needing him to go on, so fervently that she reached down to take him in her hand and guide him to her, raising her hips to meet him.

Now she had no thought of the future, or the past— only the present, here, with this man she loved. Now she thought not of morals or scandal, only trust and passion.

She would have him, as he would have her, together as man and woman were meant to be.

When he entered her, she bit her lip against the brief, sharp pain as he shoved past the tender barrier of flesh.

He paused, hesitating, looking down at her with loving concern. "I should have waited until we were married," he muttered, making as if to pull away.

She held him fast, for she had no regrets. Not now, not ever. No matter what happened. Not even if she never saw him again, although she would. He would come back to her. She was as sure of that as she was that the sun would rise, or the world would keep turning. He would be true and faithful because it simply wasn't in him to be otherwise.

As she would be true and faithful to him.

"Too late," she replied, smiling her encouragement and love. "Happily too late. I am yours forever, Gordon, whether I stay now, or go."

He smiled, and the remorse left his features. "I should have known that once you resolved to do a thing, you do it, without fear or favor. Without conditions or regrets." He kissed the tip of her nose, then each eyelid. "I pray God I never give you cause to regret this."

"You won't," she assured him as she wrapped her arms about him. "You won't."

His gaze dropped to her body beneath him—the rosy peak of her nipples and her soft, round breasts; her slim waist and flaring hips. "You're so beautiful," he murmured before he went back to pleasuring her breasts, first one, then the other and began to thrust with seemingly slow deliberation, as if to taunt her.

She met him thrust for thrust and when his speed increased, so did hers. Her lips parted as she uttered words and sounds, hardly aware of what she was saying, except that he must continue. He mustn't stop. Not yet. Oh, sweet merciful heaven, not yet.

Touch her there. And there. Oh, yes. Don't stop.

She grabbed his shoulders and half raised herself so that she could pleasure him as he pleasured her, sucking and licking his hardened nipples, letting the dark hairs tickle her nose, rejoicing as he groaned softly and pushed harder. Faster. Deeper. Each time better, stronger than the last.

It was like climbing to the highest levels of a warehouse, up and up, reaching for something just out of reach. Something wondrous, she was sure. Something like...

That!

She clenched her teeth to keep from crying out loud enough to wake the servants. She gripped his shoulders as if afraid of falling as her body pulsed. And then he shoved his mouth against her shoulder to stifle the roaring groan that rose from deep within his throat as he jerked and thrust and bucked, moving with her and in her.

Until he stopped.

Panting, he pulled back and she collapsed against the pillow, as out of breath and sweat-slicked as he. Sated and satisfied. Truly his, as he was truly hers.

He moved away a little and laid his head against her

breasts as their breathing slowed. He sounded as if he'd run a footrace—and he was supposed to rest.

"I hope I haven't hurt you," she whispered. "I didn't realize it would be quite so…so…like that."

He raised himself on his elbow to look at her and spoke with grave sincerity. "I've never felt better in my life, and I've never made a more important contract."

"Contract?" she repeated, confused.

He reached out and tucked a lock of her hair behind her ear. "Indeed. A very solemn verbal contract that we are to be husband and wife, and confirmed in a most exciting, if unusual, manner."

She frowned, some of her enjoyment of this night gone. "Even if we don't marry, I would never sue you for breach of contract."

He kissed her forehead lightly. "I'm sorry. I didn't mean to remind you of that. It's just that I'm a solicitor and tend to think in legal terms. I give you my word I won't sue you, either, should you change your mind."

"I won't," she said firmly. Then she gave him a shy little smile as she remembered how wanton and wild they both had been, and how glorious he had made her feel, and she ran her hand across his chest. "Especially after tonight."

His smile warmed her in more ways than one. "Then I trust I didn't disappoint?"

"Not in the least." She frowned. "I hope I didn't."

"Not in the least. In fact, I confess myself most pleasantly surprised," he said, stroking her arm in a way that sent both shivers and thrills of excitement through her.

She wanted nothing more than to stay, to lie beside him and spend the whole night, but that was impossible, at least for now. So it was with reluctance that she moved away from him and sat up. "I have to go, Gordon, and you have to rest."

He sat up, too. "My heart wants to argue against that statement, but my rational mind counsels me not to be foolish," he said with wry acquiescence. "Besides, I don't want to give myself a relapse. I want to be completely well as soon as possible."

"I want you to be completely well as soon as possible, too," she said as she got out of bed and picked up her discarded nightdress.

"Don't put it on just yet," he pleaded. "Let me look at you a moment longer in the firelight."

"You make me feel like an artist's model," she said, slightly abashed as he studied her.

"I want to memorize the sight of you thus," he replied. "You're like a goddess—only better, because you're mortal. I wouldn't feel competent to make love to a goddess."

"I suppose if you displeased a goddess, she could turn you into a pig or a cow," she replied. "Not that I think you would disappoint," she added as she returned his scrutiny, her gaze traveling over his naked, muscular body.

"You had better go," he said huskily as he covered himself with the sheet, "or I may forget my rational wisdom and make love with you again."

"If that's a threat, it's not a very good one," she said,

her body moist and ready again, her breasts tingling with anticipation of his touch.

His eyes flared with desire as he threw back the sheet. "Come here, Moira. Please."

She did.

"I really *must* leave this time, Gordon," Moira whispered as she slid out of his arms. "It'll be dawn soon."

Although she was right to be concerned, he sighed nonetheless, and not just because he was sorry she had to go. He was completely, utterly, wonderfully exhausted.

And completely, utterly, wonderfully happy, happier than he'd ever been—happier even than when he'd won his first lawsuit for a client. "I wish we could stay in this room all day. For a week—a month!"

"I do, too, but people would talk."

How they would! He sat up as she rose from the bed. She was so beautiful, with her hair loose about her lovely body. Exciting and intelligent, too.

Perfect.

She pulled on her thin nightgown that did little to hide her luscious curves, then picked up her bedrobe from the floor and went to the window. "The moon's bright tonight," she noted, holding her robe against her breasts.

Standing in the moonlight, the rest of her body was visible through the sheer fabric, giving him quite a view—and arousing him quite thoroughly.

"If you don't move away from that window, I'll

have no choice but to make love to you right where you are."

She half turned toward him. "Standing by the window?"

"Yes, standing by the window."

Indeed, the idea was almost irresistible. Almost, because they would be by a window and soon the servants would be stirring, including, he supposed, the gardeners.

"We couldn't!"

"No, not here, I don't suppose," he agreed. "But someday, Moira my love… Not at a window, but otherwise…"

She gasped as if horrified.

"It's not that outrageous," he said, surprised she would find the notion so completely repulsive after what they'd already done together. She'd been as wild and wanton as any man could wish, letting him—

She raised her hand and pointed out the window to the garden below, her finger shaking. "It's that dog! That big black dog and it's on the terrace! Ring for the servants!" she cried as she hurriedly tugged on her robe and ran for the door. "You'll have to say you saw it. My room doesn't overlook the terrace."

Then she was gone.

Wincing and holding his side, he climbed out of bed and went to the bellpull and gave it several tugs. Then he went the window as quickly as he could. Standing behind the drapery because he was still naked, he surveyed the terrace and the garden. He couldn't see…

Yes! There it was, just disappearing through a yew

hedge, the same huge ogre of a dog. He ran a swift gaze over the terrace, gardens and lawn, but as far as he could see, the dog had been alone.

He started to dress, until he heard the sound of footsteps rushing up the servants' stairs. Wearing only his trousers, he went to the door and saw Moira coming out of her bedroom as two footmen and her maid arrived from the servants' stairs.

A confused expression on her wide-awake face, Moira hadn't dressed, but had her bedrobe on and belted over her nightgown. "What's happened?"

"I saw the same dog I saw the night of the fire," he said to the closest footman. His jacket wasn't completely buttoned, and the flustered Walters was still tying his cravat.

"I shall alert the gamekeeper," Walters announced, turning back toward the stairs.

"And the grooms and gardeners," Moira ordered. "That dog may have a master and they must search for him, too."

As Gordon turned to go back into the room and finish dressing, Moira called out to him.

"You aren't going to help search, are you, Mr. McHeath?" she asked with obvious concern.

"No. I shall wait here, with you."

Chapter Nineteen

A short time later, dressed and shaved and having had a brief breakfast of toast and kippers, with a cup of tea to wash it down, Gordon sat beside Moira in the drawing room trying not to recline or otherwise indicate that his side was aching. She was already tense and anxious enough, and he didn't want her to blame herself for any pain he was feeling after their activities last night. He was fairly certain he hadn't done any serious damage, but he was hurting enough that it would surely be wiser to stay here than to chase after the dog.

"Why was that dog at the house?" she wondered aloud, her posture as straight and upright as if she had a spear down her dress. "Were they trying to break into the house, do you think?"

"It's no secret that the earl is rich," Gordon replied, "although Walters says there's no indication that anyone tried to get in the doors."

He wasn't going to tell her that an experienced and skilled thief would have a set of picks that would make any lock no hindrance. "It could be that the vandals fled Dunbrachie and left the dog to fend for itself. It would tie them to the attack, after all."

He hoped that was the case, but he could think of at least one other reason besides theft that those men might try to get inside the manor, one that had nothing to do with robbery and everything to do with Moira, who was now lacing and unlacing her fingers in her lap. How he wished he'd been able to capture them and turn them over to the authorities the night they set fire to the school! If only he'd been more careful or heard that man coming up behind him before it was too late.

Not wanting to lie to her, afraid to say anything more that might worsen her dread, unable to touch her in case the servants saw, and not well enough to join the search himself, all he could do was sit where he was, offering the solace of his company, and hope that was enough.

As the morning wore on, she rose and started to pace. "I suppose we should send for the constable," she remarked at midmorning.

He should have thought of that instead of dwelling on what he *couldn't* do. "Absolutely. We should let him know the dog's been seen, at least."

She turned toward him. She looked so sad and vulnerable, he wanted to hug her, although he didn't dare. "I hope you're right and they're far away," she said. "I would rather those men never get caught and punished than think of them still lurking about."

Servants be damned. He got up and went to her,

taking her in his arms and holding her gently. "I don't want to think of anyone like that anywhere near you." He voiced something he'd been thinking about since their hasty breakfast. "Perhaps you should go to Glasgow today."

"I don't have anything ready. And the grooms and drivers are out looking for the dog. That's more important, isn't it?"

He kissed her tenderly, silently agreeing. "Tomorrow then."

"I'd feel safer if you'd stay here with me and we both leave tomorrow. It's too late for you to start now anyway. At the rate Dr. Campbell wants you to travel, you wouldn't get farther than Dunbrachie."

"I'd be happy to stay. More than happy."

She leaned close and whispered, "I don't want to sleep alone tonight."

"You won't," he promised her, pulling her close to kiss.

A shot rang out in the distance.

Startled, wondering who or what had been the target, Gordon went to the window. Moira hurried to join him there.

"Can you see anything?" she asked anxiously.

"No. It came from over there," he said, nodding at the yew hedge that bordered the wood at the south side of the property.

"What do you suppose it means?"

"Only one shot could mean they saw something but missed. Or perhaps they hit their target, whatever it was, with one shot. We'll have to wait and see."

Fortunately, they didn't have to wait long. A stable boy with bed-tousled hair and a short, patched woollen jacket and equally patched trousers came running from the direction of the wood. He dashed across the terrace and entered when Moira opened the door for him.

"Jem got him, my lady!" he cried, panting. "Big brute of thing it was, too. Charged right at him like a wild boar, so he didn't have no choice."

Perhaps the dog had been abandoned, then. If that was so, if it was frightened and desperate, he could only pity the poor creature.

"Was anyone seen with the dog?" Gordon asked. "Or was anybody seen who didn't belong on the grounds?"

"No, sir, no. Just the dog."

Moira took Gordon's hand, and he could feel her trembling.

No, he wouldn't leave her here, not while there was still a chance those men who attacked him and had been paid to harass her might be nearby, with or without their dog.

"They shot Dan. They shot Dan," Charlie moaned, hugging his knees as he sat in the dim loft of the small outbuilding on the earl's estate. "We should've stayed here, let you get your own rabbit."

"Shut yer gob," Red ordered through clenched teeth, huddling to keep warm against the chill of the damp day. "It was only a dog."

Charlie glared at him. "He was smarter than you'll ever be!"

"Not smart enough not to get himself killed! And it would ha' been worse if they'd caught *us*."

"We never should have come here at all," Charlie muttered. "We should have stayed in the cave. Nay, stayed in Glasgow. I told you it was too risky, that we couldn't trust 'im. Self-made men can be worse than crooks—do ya think it's only luck? Half of 'em makes pirates look like gentlemen. But you said it'd be easy money. Like a fool I listened—and now my Dan is dead!"

"Quit yer whingin'! That wouldn't have happened if you'd kept the damn dog tied, like I told you," Red retorted.

"He wouldn't have liked it."

"He likes being dead better, I suppose."

Charlie's teeth drew back in a snarl. "He's dead because o' you and this stupid scheme that was supposed to make us rich. Well? Where's the rest o' the money? Rafe and my dog dead and we're stuck here like rats in a hole!"

Charlie got to his feet, although he had to bend to keep his head from hitting what was left of the roof. "Well, I ain't stayin'. I ain't getting caught and strung up. Bad enough I lost my dog, I ain't gonna lose my own life, too."

Red likewise rose, blocking the way to the ladder that was missing three rungs and the only way down. "If that's what you want, go ahead. More for me."

"Then get out o' my way!"

Red stepped to the side. Charlie turned to start down the ladder, his eyes looking down for the next rung.

Red stuck out his foot and shoved the ladder backward.

"Hey!" Charlie cried as it started to move and he frantically reached for something to hold on to.

He found Red's leg. Like a drowning man, he grabbed it and held on for dear life.

"Let go! Damn you, let go!" Red shouted as the ladder swayed like a drunken seaman on shore leave and he felt himself being dragged toward the edge.

There was a scream, a shout, a crash and a moan.

And then there was only silence.

Wearing only his trousers and shirt, leaning his head wearily on his hand after what felt like the longest day of his life, Gordon sat in the blue bedroom.

Had that poor beast been left behind by the vandals who'd attacked him, or were they still in the vicinity, waiting to do more mischief or even harm Moira?

Thank God Moira was leaving for Glasgow, even though he had no idea how long it would be before he saw her again.

At least his side had stopped aching….

The door to his room opened and Moira slipped inside, dressed in that same soft bedrobe and thin night-dress, her bountiful, beautiful hair undone and loose about her shoulders.

She let her robe fall from her shoulders as she crossed the room toward him and he hurried to meet her halfway.

"My Moira," he murmured as he gathered her into his arms and held her close.

"Gordon," she whispered as she raised herself on her toes to kiss him. "Take me to bed, Gordon. Take me to bed and love me and let me forget what's happened today, for a little while at least."

"Gladly," he replied, only too happy to do as she asked.

Because not only was it a joy to love her, he wanted to forget, too.

When Moira opened her eyes, a ray of sunshine was coming in through the narrow opening between the closed drapes.

That wasn't what woke her. Nor was it the singing of birds in the garden, or the cocks crowing, or the lowing of cows as they waited to be milked.

It was the chambermaid laying the coal in the blue bedroom's hearth. Moira's breath caught—until she realized that she'd fallen asleep on the far side of the bed behind Gordon and was thus hidden from the maid's view.

She should have gone to her own room immediately after they'd made love—wonderful, glorious love—but she'd been so sated and so satisfied, so comfortable and secure, she hadn't wanted to hurry away. So she'd asked him instead about his family and nestled against him as he told her of his deceased parents and their hopes and dreams for him, and the sacrifices they'd made for his education that gave him such an appreciation for her efforts to open a school. And, she had realized, put him in thrall to the popular Robbie when he was a young impressionable lad desperate to make friends at school.

She told him about her mother, who'd taught her at home until her death, and then her days at school. And the times she got to go to the warehouses with her father, and how he let her roam around and climb like a monkey—her happiest memories, until she'd met Gordon.

Afterward they'd lain in companionable silence. She'd intended to ask him about his legal education, but she'd drifted off to sleep instead.

It was a long, torturous wait for the maid to finish her task, made more tense by the fear that Gordon would wake and speak to her, or roll onto his back, or somehow reveal her presence in the bed.

At last she heard the maid rise. But instead of leaving at once, she continued to stand by the hearth. What on earth for? Moira wondered, until it occurred to her that she might simply be admiring Gordon. The sheets only covered his lower torso and legs. What woman wouldn't be tempted to take in such a view?

She felt Gordon's body tense and his breathing quicken. He must be awake, too, but he wisely didn't move, or she hoped, open his eyes.

At last, however, the maid gathered up the coal scuttle and brushes, and went out the door, closing it behind her.

Moira let out her pent-up breath as Gordon turned toward her, a wry smile on his handsome face. "That could have been most unfortunate."

"Could have been, but wasn't," she said, kissing him

lightly. "Nevertheless, I must go. My own maid will be coming to my room, and if I'm not there, she'll wonder why. She might sound an alarm and start searching for me after what happened yesterday."

Although Moira was determined to leave, she couldn't resist as he put his arm around her and pulled her close, his naked flesh against her own. "I'll miss you. I miss you already."

"I'm right here!" she protested, trying not to think about their inevitable, if temporary, parting.

"What do you think your father will say when he finds out I want to marry you?"

"And that *I* want to marry *you*," she returned. She ran her hand down his shoulder and along his side, in part to touch him, but also to ensure that he wasn't bleeding again.

Fortunately, the bandage was still dry, although the problem of her father's reaction to her future marriage to Gordon remained. "He said he wanted me to marry," she offered.

"To a solicitor?"

"He didn't say anything about my husband's profession."

"He doesn't have to. He's an earl now, Moira, and you're a lady. He no doubt thinks you should have a titled husband."

She brushed Gordon's hair from his forehead and kissed his cheek. "I don't want a titled husband. I want you." They were so close, she added, "As much as you want me right now."

He rolled her onto her back, so that he was above her,

his weight on his elbows. "I do want you now, and for the rest of my life, too."

He leaned down to brush his lips over hers, then drew back with a sorrowful smile and moved away so that she could get up. "Unfortunately, unless we want to be discovered together, you had best return to your own room, my lady, and leave me here to dress, so that I can go back to Edinburgh and begin to close my practice."

She still could hardly believe he would do that for her. "Write to me in Glasgow," she said, reluctantly rising from the bed and wrapping the coverlet about her. She went to the small desk in the far corner of the room to note her address.

"I'll be staying with—oh, no!" she cried as she saw the robe on the floor half under the bed where Gordon had kicked it as they'd stumbled, still embracing, to bed. "What if the chambermaid saw my robe? Maybe that's why she took so long!"

"I don't think so. The room was dark when she entered, and it's still fairly dim now with the drapes drawn. I confess I opened my eyes a bit to see why she hadn't left and she was…" He gave her a wry, self-deprecating smile. "Well, she was staring at me. If she suspects anything's amiss, it will be because I was blushing. I'm not used to being looked at that way."

Just as Moira had suspected, and she let out her breath in a slow sigh of relief. Then she grinned as she picked up her nightdress from the floor on her side of the bed and put it on. "You'd better get used to that, Gordon McHeath, because I intend to stare at your naked body every chance I get."

"So long as I get to admire yours at every opportunity, too."

She laughed softly, her body warming both with the thought of his scrutiny and realizing he was regarding her intently at that moment. "I really *must* go," she said again, both for his benefit and her own.

Gordon didn't try to dissuade her. After all, she was right—it would make things more difficult for them both, but especially her, if word got out that they'd shared a bed. Even so, it was difficult to watch her and realize that it could be weeks before they could be together again, let alone marry, and in that time, a host of things could happen.

Then something did.

A familiar voice came roaring from the foyer below. "I want to see them both, by God, and I want to see them now!"

Chapter Twenty

Their startled gazes met as they recognized Robbie's slurring shout before simultaneously starting for the door.

"I have to get to my room and dress," Moira said, reaching it first. "Stay here. I'll see what he wants."

"No, let me speak to him."

"I think the butler's coming upstairs," Moira whispered as she opened the door and peered into the corridor. She glanced back at him. "Whatever his reasons, Robbie has no right to come here and demand anything," she said before she slipped from the room.

She was right about that, of course, yet that probably wouldn't occur to a man like Robbie, who was used to getting his own way in everything.

So he had best make haste and get to him first. He certainly wasn't going to hide up here and leave Moira to deal with Robbie alone.

Determined to do so, Gordon got dressed as quickly as he could. Shaving would have to wait.

He was buttoning his shirt when there was a knock at the door, and he opened it to find the agitated butler.

"I'm sorry to disturb you, sir," Walters said, "but Sir Robert McStuart has arrived and wishes to speak to you at once."

That was a polite way to put Robbie's shouted demand. "Where is he?"

"The drawing room."

"Tell him I'll be down directly."

"Yes, sir."

Thankfully it would take Moira longer to dress, so hopefully he'd be able to get Robbie out of the house before she had to see him, let alone speak to him. "Is he drunk?"

Walters gravely inclined his head. "I believe he is, sir."

"Thank you, Walters."

Gordon ducked back into the room to finish doing up his shirt. That done, he abandoned his cravat and was sure he was ready before Moira. Nevertheless, when he left the blue bedroom, she was dressed and coming out of hers. She now wore a day gown of pale green muslin, and her hair had been simply coiled around her head.

"Moira, there's no need for us both to go below," he said. "He was my friend. Let me deal with him."

"I'm not a child, Gordon," she resolutely replied. "Whatever Robbie wants, it must involve me, too."

He should have known she wouldn't shirk from

facing this difficulty, either. "Very well, but according to Walters, he's drunk."

"I do have some experience dealing with drunken men," she grimly reminded him as they started toward the stairs.

How he wished she didn't! How he wished he could somehow erase that part of her past or at least make her forget anyone who had ever caused her grief.

He couldn't. All he could do was be with her and hold her hand as they went down the stairs to the drawing room, regardless of who might see them.

The butler waited just outside the drawing room door, and two more footmen stood at attention nearby.

"Reinforcements, should we require them," Moira murmured with relief as they went through the double doors.

To find Robbie in a state of extreme agitation, as jittery as any prisoner in the box Gordon had ever seen.

He wasn't alone. Standing almost in the corner was a slender, slim-featured man of indeterminate age, wearing a severely plain black jacket and trousers, his shirt white linen, his cravat simply tied, his hair slicked down and combed back from his forehead.

Pointing and glaring at them, Robbie turned to this unknown fellow and cried, "You see? They *are* in league together!"

"Robbie, calm yourself," Gordon sternly commanded as he moved forward as fast as he could, ignoring a twinge of pain in his side.

"That's fine advice coming from a traitor!" his friend declared. "How long have you been lovers? Since you were *supposedly* hurt? Or before that? Maybe you met in Edinburgh. Maybe that's why she broke our engagement."

"Breaking our engagement had nothing to do with Gordon," Moira forcefully replied. "It had everything to do with the state you're in now. I discovered you're a sot, and a philanderer. *That's* why I wouldn't marry you."

Robbie's lip curled up with scorn. "Are you going to try to tell me you aren't lovers?"

Moira drew herself up. "No, I'm not going to tell you anything that isn't any of your business."

"Robbie," Gordon began in a mollifying tone, "we can discuss this—"

"Later? No, we can't. You've played me false, Gordo. All this time, I thought you were my friend, looking out for my best interests, and instead, you're sleeping with the enemy. And don't you dare try to deny it! I saw the look in her eyes when she told me you were too sick to be moved. The hell you were! It was an excuse for you two to be together, right under everybody's noses! Well, you might have fooled them, but you can't fool me!"

And then he threw a punch at Gordon.

As Moira cried a warning, Gordon instinctively ducked the blow. The butler and the footmen rushed into the room and pinned the nobleman's arms at his sides.

"Get out!" Moira ordered, pointing at the drawing room door. "Get out of this house!"

"Not until I tell you why I've come," Robbie retorted

as he twisted and turned, trying to free himself from the servants' grasp.

"I don't care why," Moira returned. "Take him out," she ordered the footmen.

"My lady, a moment if you please," the unknown man said, stepping forward. He cut a glance at the still-struggling Robbie. "Although I can appreciate that you are quite distraught, Sir Robert, if you'll compose and pacify yourself, we shall be able to make our intentions known, and the sooner we do, the sooner we shall be able to come to terms. Mr. McHeath, there is an important matter of legal business we need to discuss."

The man had to be an attorney, Gordon thought as Robbie stopped struggling. Moira nodded at the servants, who released him and stepped back.

This was hardly the time or place for any sort of legal business, especially when Robbie was in a rage. "I don't know who you are, sir, but if Lady Moira wishes you to go—"

"I do!" she interjected.

"Then I suggest you do so. If you leave your card, she can contact you for a more appropriate interview, without Sir Robert's volatile presence."

"Gad, you *have* changed sides!" Robbie growled as he wrenched himself free. "After all I've done for you, I never thought *you'd* desert me, and over a fickle woman, too!"

"Robbie, you'd better go, and take this fellow with you," Gordon said, his hands balling into fists as he tried to contain his temper.

Moira glanced at the butler, the look a summons, and he and the footmen came forward again.

"Oh, we'll leave," Robbie retorted, "but not just yet. Go ahead, McBean, give him the papers."

The solemn McBean reached into his jacket and drew out a packet of folded foolscap.

"Not only am I maintaining my suit against Moira, I'm hoisting you on your own petard and suing you, too," Robbie declared, his expression triumphant. "As you ought to know, Gordo, old chap, the Scots have a charming little thing called the Law of Delict, which means I can take you to court for conduct that harms the interests of another. You're supposed to be representing *my* interests, not Lady Moira's. Instead, what do you do but turn traitor and try to persuade me to drop a suit I have every chance of winning, as McBean here agrees. How did she manage to get you to do that?" He ran a scornful gaze over her. "I think we all can guess."

Moira stepped toward him. "Enough of your sordid implications! Say another word like that, and I'll sue you for slander!"

She realized the moment the words left her mouth that that was not a wise thing to say. Robbie's face flushed with even more outrage.

Gordon hurried forward, getting between the two of them. "Robbie, enough. Sue me if you will—that's your right—but we'll discuss this later, when we're all more calm."

"So you aren't going to try to deny the charge? Good for you," Robbie said, his voice dripping with angry disdain. He curled his lip as he looked at Moira. "Thank

God I didn't marry you, or I would no doubt have been cuckolded within the year."

"You...you cur!" Moira cried.

"Go, Robbie, now, or I'll drag you out of here myself," Gordon warned.

"If you do, I'll have you charged with assault!"

"I'll risk it."

Gordon's coldly, fiercely spoken words made the color drain from Robbie's face.

"I'll meet you anywhere and any time you name, except here," Gordon continued, "where I hope we can talk like civilized gentlemen."

"The only place I want to see either of you ever again is in court," Robbie declared. "And let the best man win—so you're going to be broken and bankrupt, Gordo, probably within the year."

"I doubt it. I can, after all, represent myself," he replied, his rage ebbing as he remembered Robbie's financial straits. "I trust he's paid you a retainer, Mr. McBean. If not, I suggest you insist upon that immediately."

"I believe I can look after my own interests," the solicitor replied. "I also think it would be advisable, Sir Robert, if we took our leave. Quarrelling like fishwives will get us nowhere."

"I agree," Gordon said, reaching out to take Moira's hand again. "Good day, Mr. McBean."

He said nothing to Robbie while Mr. McBean made a slight bow, the very model of politeness, as if they'd just experienced a calm, rational conversation.

With a scowl, Robbie started for the door, followed

by his solicitor, until they all heard the unmistakable
sound of carriage wheels coming to a halt at the front
of the house. Walters hurried away, followed by one of
the footmen; the other remained behind, keeping an eye
on Robbie and his new attorney.

With Gordon right behind her, Moira hurried to the
window and looked to see who had arrived.

She gasped when she saw the coat of arms on the
door. "Papa! He's home!"

She was both glad and afraid. Could there have been
a worse time for him to return?

"Well, now, isn't this interesting," Robbie said with
a sneer as he turned back into the room. "Judging by
the guilt in both your faces, I gather the new-made earl
doesn't know about your little love affair. Rather selfish of you, wouldn't you say, my high-and-mighty and
oh, so judgmental lady? And not exactly proper, is it,
Gordo? It's a damn good thing McBean and I are here.
The poor man should be made aware of the viper he's
been harboring in his house."

"Robbie, say a word to my father, and you'll regret
it!"

"You heard her, McBean!" Robbie charged, turning to his solicitor. "She threatened me! Surely there's
something in the law about *that!*"

"If you leave without speaking to the earl, Robbie,"
Gordon said before McBean could answer, "I won't
contest your suit and I'll pay whatever damages you
seek."

"You heard that, too, McBean!" Robbie crowed. His
lips turned up in a cruel smile. "Maybe I'll do as you

ask, Gordo, and maybe I would rather see the earl's face when he finds out what his oh-so-wonderful daughter has been up to under his very own roof."

If Robbie or McBean expected Moira to simply stand and do nothing, they were wrong.

Her back as stiff as that of a captain on the bridge of his ship, she addressed the footmen. "Take Sir Robert out of this house by the kitchen entrance. Drag him if you have to, but get him out of here at once."

Robbie flushed bright red. "You wouldn't dare lay a hand on me." He stabbed his finger at Gordon, his whole body shaking, his voice quivering with rage. "As for you, you ungrateful wretch, I befriended you when nobody else at school would. I took you into my confidence. I treated you as an equal, and this is how you repay me?"

"You never treated me as an equal," Gordon said. "You treated me as your lackey, your prize, perhaps even your pet, but never your equal."

"I'm going to take you for every cent you've got, Gordo—every penny you earned because I took the blame for you all those years ago. But you've forgotten that, haven't you? Forgotten what you owe me between that woman's thighs."

"I haven't forgotten," Gordon returned. "I haven't forgotten how you used me to fight your battles, and made money betting on me—even here. I haven't forgotten all the jokes at my expense. I am grateful that you took the blame for that theft, but it was my hard work that got me my post as a solicitor's clerk and my own practice. I won't let you take that away from me without a fight, Robbie. But worst of all, you tried to use me to hurt Moira."

"Hurt? What do you think she did to me when she rejected me after accepting my proposal?"

"If I hurt anything, it was only your pride," Moira said. "You never loved me. You never really wanted me. All you wanted was my dowry. Because you need the money."

Robbie, staring incredulously, stumbled backward. "How did you…? Gordon! You told her?"

"I've told her nothing about your finances, Robbie."

"I don't believe you! You told her. You told her everything and now everybody in Scotland's going to know Sir Robert McStuart is bankrupt! Scorned by a woman and bankrupt!"

He reached into his jacket and pulled out a gun.

"Robbie, what are you doing with my pistol?" Gordon asked warily, shoving Moira behind him while keeping his eye on the weapon he had carried in his greatcoat from Edinburgh.

Robbie's eyes filled with tears as he put the end of the weapon to his temple. "What do you care what I do? What do you care if I live or die? You've got your career and now you've got Moira and I've got nothing. Nothing but debts and humiliation and shame."

"Robbie, please," Moira pleaded, "put that down."

"Why? It's not as if you care, either."

"I do! I don't want you to die."

Robbie's expression hardened as he turned the pistol

to point at Gordon. "I don't think you do, but you do care about him."

"What the devil is the meaning of this?" the earl demanded from the doorway.

Taken aback, Robbie half turned—and the pistol exploded in a burst of heat and flame and the smell of gunpowder. Moira screamed and McBean shrieked. Gordon threw himself at Robbie. He got one arm around his former friend and grabbed Robbie's forearm, trying to wrestle the gun from his grip.

A low groan came from the doorway as Moira rushed to her father. His face pale as paper, the earl held on to the door frame, while a splotch of red grew on the side of his neck, spreading across his white linen cravat.

"Papa!" Moira cried as she grabbed him around the waist, trying to hold him up. "Papa!"

Gordon wanted to help, but he didn't dare let go of Robbie, not until he had the gun. Holding on to Robbie's arm with all his might, he pushed him toward the wall, determined to smash his hand against it to make him let go.

Robbie dug his heels in, but his feet were on a waxed floor and the leather soles of his boots gave him no purchase. As if engaged in some sort of bizarre dance, Gordon moved him gradually backward until they reached the wall.

Gordon shoved Robbie's hand against the painted plaster. Finally Robbie dropped the gun and for one brief instant, Gordon thought he meant to surrender.

He was wrong, for when Gordon relaxed his grip for that mere moment, Robbie charged forward, knocking

Gordon off balance. As he tried to right himself, he felt a sharp, stabbing pain in his side from his wound. Robbie, half stumbling, ran for the open door past the earl lying on the ground and Moira kneeling beside him. The footmen tried to block him, but with a desperate strength, he shoved them out of the way.

"Let him go! Fetch the doctor!" Moira shouted at the footmen as they started to give chase.

His hand on his side, Gordon ran to the door. A swift glance confirmed there was nothing he could do here. The earl's eyes were closed, and his shirt was bloody, but mercifully he was breathing.

"Gordon!" Moira cried as he continued past them.

"I've got to find Robbie," he shouted over his shoulder. Whatever Robbie had done, whatever was going to happen, he didn't want Robbie to end his own life, and he was afraid that would be Robbie's next and final, desperate act.

Chapter Twenty-One

T wo drivers and more liveried footmen waited by the earl's and Robbie's carriages, clearly wondering what on earth was happening.

Two drivers and two vehicles, so Robbie must have fled on foot, either too distraught to take his carriage, or fearful that the driver would refuse to move the vehicle, even if ordered. "Where's Sir Robert?"

"He stumbled off like a madman that way," one of the drivers eagerly replied, pointing toward the yew hedge. "Hardly upright and I think he was cryin'. We heard a shot inside. What's going on, sir?"

Gordon ignored the question. "Fetch Dr. Campbell at once," he said to the earl's driver. "You go to the village with him," he ordered the footman standing beside the driver. "Find the constable and tell him the earl's been shot. Have him bring a search party here and send men to Sir Robert's. Tell him they should see that Sir

Robert doesn't leave if he comes home and he should be arrested if he's found anywhere else."

He turned to the footman who'd followed him out of the house. "Get the other footmen and grooms and stable boys and start searching the grounds for Sir Robert. Take guns, but don't shoot at him unless he draws a weapon. I doubt he has one, though."

"Aye, sir," the footman said, bobbing his head before he ran into the house.

The driver likewise nodded and climbed aboard the earl's carriage. With a cry and a snap of his whip, the carriage leaped into motion.

Keeping a hand on his aching side, Gordon started to jog after his friend, who clearly wasn't in any condition to run fast or far.

And who was going to be charged with attempted murder. Or perhaps manslaughter. He'd been drunk, after all—was still drunk as well as distraught, judging by the footprints and occasional handprints visible in the dewy grass leading to the hedge.

Gordon reached the hedge and plunged through it into the wood. It wasn't difficult to follow Robbie here, either, for there were broken branches and crushed plants, and sometimes a muddy footprint. He went up short rises and down into ditches, over rocks and rough ground, his pursuit getting more and more difficult the farther he got from the manor house. Robbie didn't seem to be headed toward his house, or the village. Perhaps he realized he would be more easily caught if he went there.

Finally, Gordon heard what sounded like a wounded

deer thrashing its way through the underbrush. Or, judging by the curses, a drunken, frightened, desperate man trying to flee.

"Robbie, stop!" he called out with what breath he could muster as he leaned against a tree, the bark rough beneath his palms. His side hurt like hell with every rasping gulp of air and his equally pain-racked legs might give out at any moment. In spite of that, he wasn't going to give up. Despite what he'd said today, he had to find Robbie and save him from himself.

As he might have been able to save him years ago, if only he'd kept in touch. If only he hadn't been so busy with his practice. If only he'd realized sooner how troubled Robbie was, and where his drinking and gambling and wenching might eventually lead him.

He pushed off from the tree to take up the chase again, now following what appeared to be a narrow path. More than once he nearly tripped over an exposed root. The third time that happened, he stopped and leaned forward, hands on his knees, the pain nearly overwhelming.

The only thing he could hear was his own labored breathing. He couldn't hear birds, or rustling leaves, either from wind or somebody running away. It was as if Robbie had vanished, or flown away.

Then he caught sight of a small, rough stone building with a peaked wooden roof nearly hidden by the foliage. It looked like a gamekeeper's outbuilding, used for storing traps and other items useful for his job, or an abandoned barn.

He began a slow trot toward it, trying to be as quiet as

he could. There were no windows, no chimney, and the roof had fallen away at the back, but there was a door.

An open door.

Wary and cautious, Gordon walked slowly toward it, keeping to the right of the entrance as he peered through the opening.

Robbie stood inside the ruined building, his back to the door, his arms limp at his sides, swaying as he stared at a large pile of what looked like clothes on the ground beneath the edge of a loft built under the roof. There were pieces of wood, too, like a broken chair. Or ladder.

Except that it wasn't clothes, Gordon realized as he, too, stared.

It was two men. The bodies of two men that Gordon immediately recognized—the men who attacked him. The men who set fire to Moira's school.

Blood pooled near the head of the man with bright red hair and beard wearing rough, patched clothes, his left arm twisted at an odd angle, legs splayed, the other arm beneath him. The other man, older, smaller, lay on his side, curled up in a ball, eyes closed, as if he'd fallen asleep.

Had Robbie somehow…?

No. The blood on their clothes had dried, so these bodies had been here for some time.

Thank God for that—and thank God they could never hurt or frighten Moira, or anybody else, again.

With a choking sob, Robbie took a step back, turned and saw Gordon.

At once his expression changed, from fear and dismay

to angry desperation. "I won't let you take me!" he cried, inching backward so that he stepped into the pool of blood. "I didn't do this!"

His demeanor changed again, to that of a pathetic, frightened child. "I didn't mean to kill Moira's father! The pistol just went off! It was an accident, Gordo! I won't go to prison! I won't! You can't make me!"

"The earl was breathing when I left him," Gordon replied, trying to keep his voice low and soothing, so that Robbie would calm down. "You must come with me. If it was an accident—"

"It was! It was, Gordon, I swear on my life. I would never hurt Moira's father, not like that. I mean, a lawsuit is one thing…I'd never…not murder. You have to believe me."

"I do. Now come away, Robbie, out of here."

"I found them like this, Gordo. They were already dead."

"I can see that by the dried blood." He decided he might never get a better chance to find out if Robbie was involved with them. "Do you know these men? Have you ever seen them before?"

"God, no! Never! Who are they? Do you—?"

A low groan escaped his throat and he stared at Gordon, wide-eyed. "They're the men who tried to kill you, aren't they?"

Robbie fell to his knees and held up his clasped hands as if begging for his life. "I had nothing to do with that, Gordon, I swear! I've never seen these men before. Please, Gordo, you have to believe me! As angry and hurt as I was, I'd never hire men to burn down Moira's school or try to hurt her, or you."

Gordon did believe him. As Robbie grovelled, humbled and pleading, Gordon was completely certain he was speaking the truth. Whatever Robbie had become, he hadn't sunk low enough to do murder, or hire men to do it for him. He hadn't been the one to bring these men here to torment Moira and burn down her school.

His relief was enormous, and now all he wanted to do was get Robbie away from here. "Let's get out of here, Robbie. Come back with me to the earl's and I'll go home with you and we can talk about what to do. You'll have to face charges, but I think—"

His eyes wide with desperate fear, Robbie nearly tripped over the short man's corpse as he backed away. "No! I can't!" he cried as he righted himself. "I won't! I won't go to prison!"

The short man he'd almost fallen over twitched. His eyes opened and his cracked lips moved, and he whispered, "For the love o' God, help…me."

He wasn't dead?

With a cry of sheer terror, Robbie rushed forward and shoved Gordon out of the way, making for the door.

Gordon landed heavily on one knee and before he could get up, the short man reached out to grab his trouser leg.

"For…God's…sake…" he whispered, "have mercy."

Gordon wanted to go after Robbie, but he couldn't leave this man here, not like this, no matter what he'd done. And he—Gordon—was exhausted and in pain. How far and how fast could he follow, anyway? Besides,

Robbie was panic-stricken and in no state to think clearly; he should be easy to find by men more fit than he.

"I won't leave you," he said to the injured man, his decision made to leave the chase to others. He got to his feet and looked around, spying a bucket half-full of water in the corner. He dragged it over to the man and, making a cup with his hands, put them to his lips to drink.

The man slurped weakly, then lay back and closed his eyes with a sigh. His chest rose and fell again. And once more.

"Mr. McHeath!"

A breathless footman stood panting on the threshold. "Are you hurt, sir?" he asked, still in the doorway as if afraid to venture farther inside.

"No more than before," Gordon said as he rose. He gestured at the man on the ground, who was still breathing, if barely. "This man is gravely injured. Help me get him back to the manor house."

As the footman came forward, Gordon said, "The earl…?"

"They've laid him on one of the sofas and they're waiting for the doctor."

With trembling fingers and paying no heed to the blood seeping into the fine damask sofa, Moira worked to remove her father's cravat as he lay in the drawing room. His breathing was short and shallow, his face as pale as clean wool, his lips a sickly blue and he moaned a little as she worked.

At least he's alive, she kept telling herself, biting her

lip as she finally got the knot undone and pulled the linen away, exposing an ugly gash.

It was only a gash. Thank God, only a gash.

And the doctor would be here soon. Walters said Gordon had sent one of her men to bring him. And more to look for Robbie.

Using the handkerchief she took from her father's jacket pocket, she dabbed at the raw, red, long wound oozing blood. Mercifully the bullet hadn't gone into his neck.

Relieved about her father, her thoughts turned to Gordon. Surely he would be back soon, with or without Robbie, but he probably shouldn't even walk far, let alone give chase.

"Moira," her father whispered.

She dabbed at the wound again and leaned close. "Yes, Papa?"

His eyes were still closed as his fingers wrapped around her hand. "I'm sorry. So sorry."

For what? For their quarrel? For withdrawing his support for her school? For drinking? Whatever the reason for his apology, she gently replied, "It's all right, Papa. Just lie still until the doctor gets here."

He opened his bleary eyes. "I'm dying, Moira, and before I do, I have to tell you…"

"You're not dying," she assured him. "The bullet only grazed your neck."

His grip tightened. "I'm dying and I can't die with this on my conscience. I did it, Moira." He closed his eyes and as he opened them again, swallowed hard. "I hired those men to burn down your school."

She dropped his hand as if it were aflame. "You?" she gasped, unable to believe what he was saying. "That can't be. You supported my efforts, at least until recently."

"I thought you'd give up…when the villagers… Big Jack MacKracken and the others… Should have known better. You're so stubborn…I had no other choice. I had to stop you somehow," he whispered, his eyes closing.

"Setting fire to my school was bad enough, but those men nearly killed Gordon!"

"I didn't know…he wasn't supposed to be there. But you were in danger, too. So much opposition…I was so afraid. I wanted to stop you, to save you, as I saved you from Sir Robert."

She stared at him, aghast. "Those things you told me about Robbie…it was the truth, wasn't it?"

"Aye, it was true. All of it. I could have kept it secret, let you marry him. But I want you to be safe. Safe and happy. Happy like your mother and me."

She didn't know what to think, or say. Her father loved her and wanted to keep her safe, but to burn down her school… To hire those men. To cause such fear and injury. "Oh, Papa, why didn't you just talk to me?"

"No time to convince you. You're too stubborn, like me." He grimaced and shifted, and stifled a low moan. "I'm dying, Moira."

"No, you're not," she assured him, taking hold of his hand. "It's only a graze."

She heard a commotion at the entrance to the house. It had to be either the doctor or, please God, Gordon returning safe and sound. "When the doctor comes, he'll tell you so. Rest, Papa, and keep still. I'll be back in a moment," she said as she hurried from the room.

It wasn't Gordon. It was Dr. Campbell, his forehead furrowed with concern as he handed his hat and great-coat to Walters, who was temporarily holding his black bag.

"Ah, my lady!" Dr. Campbell said when he saw her coming quickly toward him. "Where is your father?"

"In the drawing room. It appears the bullet only grazed his neck."

To her surprise, that didn't seem to make the doctor any less worried. "Thank you, my lady. I'll examine him in the drawing room, then he should be taken upstairs. In his condition, any trauma to the body can be dangerous."

Taken aback by his words, she laid her hand on his arm to detain him. "What do you mean, his condition?"

"He still hasn't told you?"

Moira tried to be calm, but her heart was racing as if it wanted to escape her chest. "Told me what?"

That wasn't all that baffled her. "He's been to see you?"

The doctor regarded her with sympathy and pity, too. "Yes, although with obvious reluctance. Unfortunately, his condition is already too far advanced for me to be of any help, I regret to say. He has a progressive, painful growth in his abdomen for which there is no treatment. All I can do is try to make him comfortable. Despite my advice, he's refused to accept laudanum, claiming he could manage on his own. I think we both know how he's tried to do that, and I doubt with much success."

"Is he…do you mean he's really dying?"

"I'm afraid so, my lady. I confess I'm amazed that he's been able to hide his illness from you this long."

He had because she'd been too selfish, getting involved with Robbie and thinking about her school, and then too consumed with desire for Gordon McHeath to pay attention to the man who'd given her so much, and whom she'd repaid so poorly. All this time, she'd assumed his drinking to excess was weakness of character. Instead, her father was dying and he'd been drinking because he was sick and in pain.

"He always tries to protect me and I've been too busy with my own concerns," she said, choking back a sob, her heart full of guilt and remorse and regret as her future altered yet again—in a way as different from happily learning the true depth of Gordon's feelings as cake was from haggis.

"If you'll excuse me, my lady, I'll examine him now. I think it would be best if you weren't in the room. Your father will be less likely to make light of his symptoms," the doctor said quietly.

Without waiting for her to reply, he left Moira alone in the hallway and went into the drawing room.

Chapter Twenty-Two

Dismayed, distraught, worried about her father and concerned about Gordon, wondering what would happen if and when Robbie was caught, Moira wandered down the corridor, her steps instinctively taking her to her morning room.

For so long, until they'd come to Dunbrachie, it had been only her father and her. She remembered their happy times together in Glasgow, before he inherited a title he'd never known he had any right to. Before she'd met Robbie McStuart, or Gordon.

She couldn't leave her father now. Her school would have to wait. Her future with Gordon would have to wait. She hoped he would understand. Surely he would understand.

She walked to the window and looked out at the vast lawn and garden and wood beyond. She would trade all this if her father could be well again.

And then she saw Gordon coming around the yew hedge, walking slowly and holding his side. She didn't care that he was alone, or wonder where Robbie was as she threw open the door leading to the garden and rushed out to meet him. "Gordon!"

He held out his arms and she ran into his embrace, nevertheless taking care of his obviously sore side. "What happened? Are you in a lot of pain?"

"I'm all right, just tired and rather sore."

"You shouldn't have run after him!"

"Never mind that," he replied. "Your father...?"

She wanted to tell him everything then and there, about her father's illness and that he was responsible for the fire and everything else, but more than that, she wanted to be sure Gordon would be well. "The doctor is with him, and when he's finished, Dr. Campbell can see you, too. In the meantime, you must lie down and rest."

"Soon," he said, taking her hand as they walked slowly toward the manor house. "I must tell you about Robbie."

Although she was anxious to hear about that, Robbie's fate was less important than Gordon's health. "That can wait if you're tired."

"I'm not too tired to tell you what happened," he replied as they entered the morning room and sat together on the sofa. "I caught up to Robbie, in a tumbledown building in the wood."

"Then you made him come back with you? Where is he?"

He shook his head and sighed. "No, he got away from me again."

"How? By hurting you?" She jumped to her feet. "Let me call the doctor."

Gordon reached out and grabbed her hand before she could. "He knocked me down, but that wasn't the only thing that made it possible for him to get away. There was another man already there and he was seriously injured. I stayed with him."

"Another...? Who? What was he doing there?" she asked as she sank back onto the sofa.

"One of the men who attacked me and burned down the school, I think the one who was the dog's master. That red-haired fellow was there, too, but he was dead."

"Dead?" she gasped, trying to make sense of what he was telling her. "How? Did Robbie...?"

"If anybody had a hand in it, it wasn't Robbie. He was as stunned as I when we came upon them lying on the ground," Gordon replied.

He took hold of her hand in both of his. "It looks as if they were up in the loft of the building and fell. The red-haired man must have broken his neck. The other man has broken ribs and one of his hips was dislocated. We brought him back here. The doctor should examine him, as well, although I don't think there's much that can be done. I think the internal damage was severe and he'd been lying there too long."

"Oh, Gordon!" she cried softly, her voice trembling. This was terrible to hear, but she had something to tell him, too, and she would, as difficult as it was. "My father paid those men to destroy my school."

For a moment, Gordon simply stared at her in stunned silence. "Why?" he finally asked.

"He told me he was worried that the people who were against my school might try to hurt me. He wanted me to stop, but didn't think he could convince me, so instead he hired those men."

She pulled her hand away and rose, pacing in front of Gordon, too upset to sit. "I knew he was concerned about my safety. I was aware that he feared my idea for a school in Dunbrachie was going to cause trouble for me. I even knew he feared it would prevent me from finding a suitable husband—but I never, *ever* imagined he would go so far as to burn it down!"

"A misguided effort indeed," Gordon agreed, wincing slightly as he rose to face her.

"Perhaps it was the drinking that made him think that a good plan," he said with quiet sympathy.

"He wasn't drinking because he was worried about that. He was overimbibing because…" She drew in a deep shuddering breath before continuing, for it was so difficult to face this next truth, let alone speak of it. "Because he's dying. There's a growth in his abdomen. Dr. Campbell told me so when he came today. He wanted my father to take laudanum, but he refused. The doctor thinks he's been drinking to dull the pain instead. And all this time, I was condemning him for weakness, for being selfish, for breaking his promise, when I should have seen…or asked…"

His own fatigue and pain forgotten in light of her

anguished distress, Gordon put his arms about her and held her close.

"Oh, Gordon, I said such terrible things to him!" she whispered, her voice breaking.

He had heard that sort of dry-throated remorse, the guilt, the sorrow, many times in his practice.

"Don't blame yourself," he said softly, his lips against her hair. "I suspect that even if you had asked him if he was sick, he would have denied it. I've met other men like your father, who think silence is better than revealing the truth, who believe that by keeping their illness or troubles to themselves, they spare their loved ones fear and worry. They don't realize that ignorance can cause more worry and pain, and their efforts to be stoic can lead to havoc and misunderstanding when they're gone. Yet I'm sure that in his heart he wanted to spare you, because he loves you."

His words touched her heart and lifted the worst of the burden of guilt and regret from her. She leaned against him, gaining strength from his strength, and consolation not just from his words, but from his presence, and his love.

"He thought he was protecting me," she agreed, "just as he was protecting me from a bad marriage when he told me about Robbie."

"Do you think it would help if he knows he doesn't have to worry that you'll be alone? That there is another man who loves you deeply and who'll try to keep you safe and happy for the rest of your life? Who can hardly wait for the day he can call you his wife?"

As happy as that thought made her, she didn't

immediately agree. "Considering how he feels about you, it might be best not to speak of our plans, at least not right away. Perhaps in a few days."

"Whenever you think best," he said, stroking her cheek.

She took his face between her hands and kissed him slowly, tenderly.

As she wanted to—and would—kiss him every day of her life.

A few hours later, the constable stood in the earl's drawing room, twisting his hat in his hands and shaking his head as he addressed Moira and Gordon.

"We've searched everywhere and questioned every innkeeper, livery stable owner, postilion and tollbooth keeper between here and Edinburgh, and as far north as Inverness and halfway to Glasgow and Stirling, too. Nobody's seen him. Only sign of Sir Robert has been the coat on the beach up near Plockton, like I said."

Moira and Gordon exchanged wary, dismayed glances.

"You're certain there was no boat there?" Gordon asked.

"No, sir, none, according to the fishermen who use that stretch of sand."

"Oh, Gordon," Moira said, trying not to cry. In spite of everything Robbie had done and all the anguish he'd caused, she didn't want to believe he was dead.

"Aye, my lady, it's a bad business when a body does himself in, but that looks to be the way of it. Sir Robert walked into the ocean and never came out."

Mr. McCrutcheon cleared his throat and his manner became more professional and less like an undertaker offering solace to the bereaved. "To the other matter, about the fire. Since all the men responsible are dead and we never did find out who paid them, there isn't much we can do in the way of prosecution, I'm afraid."

Moira and Gordon exchanged glances. Knowing the truth themselves and given her father's condition, they had decided not to enlighten the constable, at least not as long as her father still lived.

"We're satisfied knowing that they won't be setting any more fires," Moira said.

"Aye, well, that they won't. Now, about the inquest, Mr. McHeath. The coroner thinks there's no need for you to come back to Dunbrachie to give evidence. He says that man we thought you killed wasn't killed at the school at all, so there's no chance you did it. He'd been dragged a ways, you see."

"How can you tell?" Moira asked, pleased that Gordon needn't testify, but surprised by the constable's explanation, too.

"The mud on his clothes, and it was matted in his hair. Too much of it, the coroner says. Never occurred to me to take that into account, I'm sorry to say, but then, by the time I usually see a body, the family's washed it."

Mr. McCrutcheon put his hands on his knees and hoisted himself to his feet. "Yes, it seems like the three of 'em managed to do each other in. Pity more bad 'uns don't do the same, but then what are prisons for, eh?

"I'll be off now then," he continued when they didn't

reply. "I'd say it was a pleasure, Mr. McHeath, but that doesn't seem quite right under the circumstances."

"I can say it was a pleasure to meet you, though," Gordon said, rising to shake his hand. "You'll let us know if you hear anything more about Sir Robert?"

"Aye, sir, aye," he affirmed. "Well, good day. And here's hoping the next time we meet, it's under more sociable conditions."

Gordon nodded, then turned back into the room, where Moira stood looking out the windows at the garden. The day was gray and gloomy, but she was like a ray of sunlight against the windowpanes.

"Do you believe Robbie's dead?" she asked when he came up behind her and wrapped his arms about her.

"Without any other evidence, it's difficult to say what happened. I'd like to think he simply went to the shore to think, removed his jacket and forgot it when he left, but when I recall how he was the last time I saw him—" Gordon shook his head "—it's difficult to be optimistic."

"I'm so sorry I ever agreed to marry him," Moira said with a heavy sigh. "How much pain and trouble for all of us could have been averted if I'd known my own heart better and not let my pride and vanity sway me!"

"We're all liable to pay heed to our pride and vanity," Gordon said softly. "If I hadn't, I wouldn't have been so thrilled when Robbie paid attention to me when I was young. I would have seen his flaws and realized I should avoid him. If I had known my own heart better, I would have realized that what I felt for a certain young woman in Edinburgh wasn't love, or even desire. It was just boyish admiration."

He pulled Moira back against him. "Now that I know what love is, I know I was a fool to think that what I felt for Catriona was even close."

Moira turned in his arms, so that they were face-to-face. "I've been thinking, Gordon, and I've decided to tell my father about us today. There have been too many secrets already."

Gordon studied her determined features. "Are you quite sure?"

"Quite. Besides, I'd like him to be at our wedding. And I think it should be…soon."

"Today would suit me admirably," Gordon sincerely replied, "but if I must wait a few more days, so be it."

She gave him a wistful smile. "I would rather it be today, too, but you must have some time to return to Edinburgh and see your clients."

"I also have to prepare for the move to Dunbrachie. And I should inform my friends they're going to be receiving wedding invitations."

"I hope your friends like me."

"Well," he said slowly as he sat on the sofa and drew her down onto his lap, "I confess I haven't given much thought to any socializing we may be doing. I've been thinking about being alone with my wife."

"I've thought about being alone with my husband, too," she confessed as she wound her arms around his neck.

His lips quickly found hers, and they shared a kiss.

"Good God!"

Moira sprang up from the sofa and turned to see her father standing indignantly on the threshold.

"Papa!" she cried, hurrying toward him, surprised and upset, but not because she'd been caught kissing Gordon. "What are you doing out of bed? The doctor said—"

"Bother the doctor!" he interrupted. "I know when I'm well enough to get out of bed—and it's a damn good thing I did, too, when this is what I find!" He pointed at Gordon, who had also gotten to his feet. "Get out of my house, you…you rogue!"

Moira put her hands on her father's outstretched arm, gently forcing it lower. "Please, Papa, you don't understand."

"The hell I don't! I saw what he was doing!"

"What I was doing, too, Papa," she said as she faced him. "There's no need to be angry. We're going to be married."

The earl's eyes widened as he stared at her, then Gordon, then his daughter again. *"Married?"* he repeated, as if she'd announced she was getting a tattoo.

"Married," she confirmed. "As soon as possible."

"Are you with child?" he demanded.

"No, Papa!" she cried, aghast and suddenly sorry she'd announced their plans. But she had, and there was no going back now. "We're in love and we're going to be married. You wanted me to be a wife, didn't you? Well, now I will be."

"Yes, but…but…" Her father felt for the sofa and sat heavily. He glanced up at Gordon, then turned his stern gaze back to Moira. "Have you somehow forgotten that this man was helping Robert McStuart to sue you?"

"*Was,*" Gordon emphasized. "I'm no longer his solicitor, or his friend."

If her father hadn't been so sick, Moira would have pointed out that the earl had done worse by hiring men to burn down her school, but since he was ill, and because she was sure Gordon could argue his own case without her help, she stayed silent.

"You're only a solicitor. You're not even a barrister."

"That's true," Gordon replied evenly. "However, I make a very good living and am well respected in my profession. And I promise you, my lord, that your daughter's welfare and happiness will always be my first consideration."

"As well as our children's," Moira added.

Her father continued to scowl, but she saw cause for hope in his eyes. "Children will keep you at home, at least," he muttered, giving her a sidelong glance before he eyed Gordon speculatively. "I don't suppose you can make her give up these notions about education for the poor."

"I don't intend to try. Indeed, my lord, I intend to help her in any way I can."

"Huh."

"My lord, I appreciate that your objections stem from a natural urge to protect your child," Gordon said in what Moira could only assume was his courtroom timbre, "yet

I must point out that she is legally an adult. You cannot forbid her marriage nor her charitable endeavors."

His voice and expression softened. "Besides, my lord, you must realize you've raised a woman as determined and clever as yourself."

Moira doubted there could have been anything better Gordon could have said to mollify her father.

"You'll have to live in Edinburgh, I suppose," the earl grumbled.

"No, Papa, I still want my first school to be here," Moira said.

"I understand there is a lack of legal representation in Dunbrachie and the surrounding area," Gordon said quickly before her father realized she'd said her *first* school, "whereas solicitors are rather thick on the ground in Edinburgh. So we plan to live in Dunbrachie, provided I can find a suitable house."

Finally her father's shoulders relaxed, and he even smiled. "In that case, I have no objections," he allowed, "but what is this about finding a house when there is this huge place? It would be a waste of money to buy another. It will be yours one day anyway, Moira. You both might as well live here."

He then shook a finger at Gordon and declared, "Keep a tight rein on her, my lad, or she'll run rough-shod all over you! She's just like her mother—a head full of ideas and plans and schemes." He lowered his hand and his expression grew tender as he regarded his daughter. "But if you love her half as much as I loved her dear mother, you'll be a very happy fellow."

"Oh, Papa!" Moira cried as she threw her arms around him and smiled through her tears.

Some weeks later, Moira looked up and smiled when she saw her husband standing on the threshold of the drawing room in the manor house of the earl of Dunbrachie.

Her smile faded when she saw his weary, worried expression.

Setting aside the garment she was sewing, she hurried to kiss Gordon lightly on the lips. "Did Mr. MacIntosh prove to be even more stubborn about the contract than you feared?"

The cantankerous Mr. MacIntosh and his complicated business affairs had been consuming much of Gordon's time and effort in his new practice.

"No," he replied as he wrapped his arms around her.

"You had another client who wanted to talk about your victory over the Titan of Inverness?"

"No," he replied with a bit of a smile. "I suppose I shouldn't complain if that sends clients to my door, but it does get a little tiresome."

She thought of something that might erase that grim expression from his face.

"Dr. Campbell said my father's doing much better than expected," she said as she led him to the sofa and drew him down beside her. "Keeping him away from drink and having Mrs. McAlvey's help has been very beneficial. Dr. Campbell thinks that if things continue this way, my father may live for at least another eight months—certainly long enough to see his first grandchild."

"I'm glad he's…" Gordon paused and his visage became a stunned blank for a moment. Then his eyes lit up with a joy that lifted her happiness to new heights, too.

"Grandchild!" he exclaimed as he jumped to his feet as if she'd poked him with the fire tongs—and he liked it. "Moira! Are you…are we…a baby?"

"Yes, we're having a baby," she laughingly confirmed.

He pulled her up and into his arms before kissing her face, all over. "Oh, Moira!" he gasped between kisses. "This is wonderful! I couldn't be happier. Or feel more blessed."

For several minutes, they embraced and kissed and held each other. Moira clung to him tightly, loving him, loving the life they shared after all they'd been through.

So when Gordon eventually pulled away, she was taken aback to see that he looked even more gravely serious. "I'm so happy, I nearly forgot. I've had news about Robbie."

No wonder he had looked so serious! "Is he… dead?"

"No, he's alive."

"Alive?" she gasped, relieved and yet not quite willing to believe it. "Where is he? Has he been caught? Is he in prison?"

Her husband took her hand. "Sit down, Moira,

please, and I'll explain," he said, and she obeyed, barely realizing where she was sitting.

He sat beside her and pulled an envelope from his jacket. "I received this letter this afternoon. It's from Robbie himself. He's somewhere in America. He's sorry for everything that happened, and regrets causing us any pain or heartache."

"I'm glad he's not dead," Moira replied with heartfelt relief and sincerity. "But his coat…or was that someone else's?"

"No, it was his. He was going to drown himself, but at the last moment, the tide turned and he took it as a sign that he, too, could turn the tide of his life—and he has.

"He enclosed a document giving me power of attorney over his entire estate. He's instructed me to sell all his property and the mill to pay off his debts. If there's any money left after that, I am to give it to you to use in the building of a school. He wants nothing for himself."

"Nothing? But how will he live?"

Gordon drew the letter out of his jacket pocket, opened it and read:

"I want nothing because I deserve nothing. I've done terrible things that I regret more than I can say. I would say it cost me the best woman in the world, but she's far better off with you, Gordon, than she would have been married to a weakling like me. So I am starting over here in this new world, with a new name, and working to earn my bread. I can't say it's enjoyable, but already I feel more of a man here than I ever did in Scotland.

"I only hope you can both forgive me. Whether you do or not, I wish you every happiness and many joyful years together."

As Gordon silently folded the letter, Moira put her hand on his arm. "I'm glad he's alive, Gordon, and I think we can be hopeful that he'll be all right. Perhaps," she added softly, "he'll find a good woman to love and have a family, too."

"I'd like to think so," Gordon said, tucking the letter back in his jacket. "After all, if it weren't for Robbie, I'd never have been traveling along that road and found a beautiful young woman taking refuge in a tree."

"I'm thankful, too," Moira said as she looked into his eyes shining with love. "If he hadn't invited you here, I would never have met the love of my life. I love you so much, Gordon McHeath!"

"As I love you, my lady," he replied, as he bent his head to kiss her.

* * * * *